DAT'S LOVE
AND OTHER STORIES

Leonora Brito was born on July 7 1954. Her mother was from Cardiff's docklands and her father was a seaman from the Cape Verde Islands. Brito left school at sixteen, and it wasn't until she was in her twenties that she attended college, taking a foundation art course followed by a degree in Law and History at Cardiff University. In 1991, she won the Rhys Davies Short Story Prize and her début short story collection, *Dat's Love*, was published in 1995. She was working on a second collection at the time of her death in 2007.

DAT'S LOVE
AND OTHER STORIES

LEONORA BRITO

PARTHIAN
LIBRARY OF WALES

Parthian, Cardigan SA43 1ED
www.parthianbooks.com www.thelibraryofwales.com
The Library of Wales is a Welsh Government initiative which highlights and
celebrates Wales' literary heritage in the English language.
Published with the financial support of the Welsh Books Council.
www.thelibraryofwales.com
Series Editor: Dai Smith
First published in 1995
© The estate of Leonora Brito
Library of Wales edition published 2017
Foreword © 2017 Francesca Rhydderch
ISBN: 9781910901212
Cover design by Lucy Llewellyn
Cover image: Joan Baker, *Warm and Cool*, c.1960, oil on canvas, 61x50cm,
University of South Wales © Joan Baker, photograph courtesy of University of
South Wales Typeset by Elaine Sharples
Printed and bound in the EU by Pulsio Sarl

LIBRARY OF WALES

CONTENTS

CONTENTS

FOREWORD

Dat's Love, first released by Seren in 1995 and now re-issued by Parthian in the Library of Wales series accompanied by two additional stories, was the single collection published by the exceptionally talented Leonora Brito. Some of these short fictions were broadcast on Radio 4, and the title-story, which won the Rhys Davies Short Story Award in 1991, was also anthologised by Susan Hill in *The Penguin Book of Contemporary Women's Short Stories*. At the time of her death in 2007, Brito was working towards another collection of stories.

Leonora Brito was born in Tiger Bay, Cardiff, on July 7 1954. Her mother and grandmother were from Cardiff, while her mother's father and her own father were seamen from the Cape Verde Islands. Many of Leonora's stories hark back to the people and places of an earlier generation. 'Dat's Love', one of her most popular and enduring pieces, about an aspiring young singer who works in a cigar factory, is typical in this respect, bringing together two of Leonora's central concerns: music, which blares powerfully at the reader from the first line of the story (*'Dat's love, tra la, la, la, dat's love'*), and the interior monologue of a young working-class black woman on the cusp of adulthood. The Cardiff Leonora wrote about was her grandmother's Cardiff: the Docks, Butetown, Tiger Bay – local ground which she recalled in her memoir-essay 'Staying Power' as 'not [...] the dangerously exotic, nefarious and essentially fictional place so often conjured up by (mainly) male writers for popular consumption'. For Brito, this was 'an altogether more mundane spot that resembled if anything a friendly, spiteful, gossipy, yet neighbourly, village'.

It was in this 'village' that Brito was born, in the family's two-room lodgings on Christina Street. The house was shared with the family's Malayan landlord, Kaddi, and 'another young family, headed by a seafarer named Limbo who practised becoming a jazz trombonist in between trips'. Leonora, or Lee, as she was known to her family, was the eldest of six. Soon after her younger sister Rose was born in 1958, the growing family put their belongings on the back of a van and left Tiger Bay, along with many other families who were being moved out to the new housing estate at Llanrumney: 'I'd just turned five on the bright summery day we left the Docks,' Brito later wrote. 'I don't remember any tears, only a mood of excitement and adventure as my brother and I were hoisted onto the back of Billy Douglas's open lorry and deposited in the family armchairs, one apiece.' Her short story 'Gone for a Song' is a resonant account of life on an estate similar to the one in Llanrumney, hinting at a mother's possible infidelity while the father is away. Like 'Dat's Love', it is a story that begins with music, followed by images exploding with vivid colours, all narrated in a strong first-person present tense voice: 'It's white lime it is, he's throwing,' a young girl says of her next-door neighbour, who is singing the tune to 'Only the Lonely' to himself as he walks up and down the garden scattering the lime over a hitherto neglected patch of earth. 'And it stays on top of the brown soil where he's dug it over, like icing sugar on a wedding cake, white.'

In an interview with Brito in 2003, fellow writer Charlotte Williams drew attention to another moment in the same story, when the narrator sees a herd of cattle in the field next to the estate – 'fifteen Africas painted in ink on their creamy white backs, like maps'. Williams wondered if this inscription of 'not only black but Africa' on the Welsh countryside was a conscious statement. 'Is the Welsh landscape part of you?' she asked. Brito's reply was both honest and laconic: '"Gone for a Song" is situated in a kind of borderland between the city proper and the countryside. The actual locality is the Llanrumney housing estate. We were black and we lived there, as did lots of other black families, so I was simply describing that. The Welsh landscape doesn't loom large in my idea of myself.'

Although she was quick to avoid mythologizing or romanticizing the places where she lived in Cardiff, Brito admitted that Tiger Bay, the 'village' where she had been born, was even then beginning to exert a strong personal and creative pull on her: 'As kids going about our daily business we were subjected to constant casual name-calling from other kids, what is now termed racial abuse,' she wrote in 'Staying Power'. 'We learned to hit back, but by the time I reached junior school I began to harbour a secret dream of one day returning to live down the Docks, where life would be miraculously happy and uncomplicated.'

While the family continued to frequent Tiger Bay to see their relatives, they didn't live there again. Instead, they moved closer to the centre of Cardiff, to Cathays, where Leonora attended St Cadoc's Roman Catholic Primary School, followed by Lady Mary's Secondary Modern. It was becoming clear to her parents that she was a bookish, creative child who loved writing and painting, and was doing well at school. Her mother went to see the headmaster of Lady Mary's to make a timid request for Leonora to be moved over to a grammar school, but according to Leonora's sister Rose she was met with a flat refusal.

When Brito left school at sixteen, she took various office jobs, and it wasn't until she was twenty-one that she enrolled at art college to do a foundation course. None of Leonora's artworks has survived, but the vivid, almost cinematic quality in her writing surely owes something to her training in Fine Art, and it would have been fascinating to explore the cross-fertilization between her paintings and stories. In 'Stripe by Stripe', for example, Brito sketches a scene with just a few bold strokes: 'At around about half-past five, two black boys crossed over the back yard of the maisonettes and headed towards the pub. It had been a very hot day, the sky was still a hazy blue, but the boys were dressed for evening, in black jackets and trousers, frilled white shirts and black bow-ties. From the veranda, Mrs Offiah watched them go.

Like a double act, the boys ducked their marcelled heads beneath the empty washing lines, once, twice, three times, then straightening up together they leapt, high over the trampled-down part of the wire netting, and disappeared around the side of the "Blue Bayou".'

When Brito graduated and returned to her office work, it was as a writer, and not an artist, that she persisted with her creative endeavours. In her mid-twenties, she changed direction again, to follow a degree in Law and History. Professor Dai Smith, editor of this series, taught her at Cardiff University, and his memories of her are one of the few glimpses we have of Leonora at this time in her life: 'Leonora Brito took a third-year course I taught in the early 1980s at Cardiff University on Culture and Society in Britain from 1880 to 1920. In these classes she was painfully shy, either resolutely silent when others intervened or herself monosyllabic in reply, almost aggressive in her assumed diffidence. I struggled to engage her, to get to know her, and began to wonder if this Joint Honours Law and History student had stumbled onto my maverick course by mistake. Then she submitted an essay on *Tess of the d'Urbervilles*. It was a revelation – insightful, objectively researched, brilliantly executed in argument and delivery. She took no obvious delight in her First Class mark for it or my unstinting praise. In her Finals, she had a very mixed bag of results. The Law was not for her. Nor yet the desiccation of historical scholarship. But she was clearly the real deal. A writer.'

Brito was unemployed for a year or so after that, and although she was naturally a solitary person who lived alone and enjoyed her own company, there was, it seems to me, in this period of her life an element of her own portrayal of a young woman living with her parents in 'Michael Miles Has Teeth Like a Broken-down Picket Fence'. What makes this visual, visceral story so powerful is the dislocating angst that permeates the ending, when news comes through that Kennedy has been shot. The narrator's mother and father are deflated because the film they had been planning on watching isn't going to be broadcast now, and they don't quite know what to do with their evening. The final scene has a scarred, existential loneliness to it that stays with the reader: 'Her mother raked what was left of the fire with the poker and asked Lesley-Ann to bring her the teapot from the kitchen. Then, her mother stood by the grate, one hand on the small of her back as if she was tired, and poured. A terrible hissing noise rose up from the cinders, and specks of ash flew from the fireplace and around the room. Lesley-Ann flailed her arms in front of her face like a wild thing, fighting off the ash, but her parents stood quite calmly, waiting for the air to clear.' In a collection from which legions of strong, loud, exuberant voices reverberate off the page, this is a moment that, when the hissing of the cinders has faded, is unusual for its silence.

Despite the strong sense of place in Brito's stories, there are several pieces in *Dat's Love* which show her expanding beyond the square mile of her home turf. Her historical short fiction 'Dido Elizabeth Belle – A Narrative of Her Life (Extant)' is an examination of the British Empire in miniature, explored through the character of the illegitimate daughter of a female African slave and her English master, one Sir John Lindsay. 'In Very Pleasant Surroundings' is an example of a quite different piece, in which Brito pushes out beyond the boundaries of naturalism: this story of a woman's final days in a hospice wraps itself around its central character in the form of scraps and snatches of literary quotations, reminding the reader that the short story is a construction of reality as well as a representation of it.

Although Brito was a little suspicious of what she thought of as the literary establishment, she was rightly proud of her achievement as a Rhys Davies prize-winner, and this moment of validation in 1991 was a turning-point for her. She gave up her job with the Welsh Water Board and embarked on a career as a full-time writer, which she combined with occasional freelance work as an editor and scriptwriter. *Dat's Love* was published by Seren in 1995, who commissioned a second collection from her. Rose remembers how much happier her sister was once she was able to devote herself to her writing, and although Leonora died before the collection could be completed, on June 14 2007, some of the stories that would have gone into it were published in magazines and anthologies. Two of these, 'Mama's Baby, Papa's Maybe' and 'Jumpshot', are included in this Library of Wales volume.

Some might think it sad that Leonora Brito didn't enjoy greater acclaim during her lifetime, but she was a writer who knew herself, knew her worth, and knew that it was the work itself that mattered, the characters and stories whose voices she threw so brilliantly on the page. What matters now is the need to keep those voices alive.

Thanks to Rose Purchase, née Brito, Leonora's sister and literary executor, for sharing her memories of Leonora with me, and to Professor Dai Smith for recalling her days as a student. Other biographical material is taken from 'Staying Power' by Leonora Brito in Cardiff Central: Ten Writers Return to the Welsh Capital *(ed. Francesca Rhydderch, Gomer, 2003), and* New Welsh Review 62, Winter 2003, *'From Llandudno to Llanrumney: Inscribing the Nation'.*

DAT'S LOVE

Dat's love, tra la, la, la, dat's love — remember that song? Well she won't be singing *that* at the funeral. In fact, although the crowds have gathered like moths around this candle-lit church, just to hear her sing, Sarah Vaughan won't be singing at Dooley Wilson's funeral at all.

I will, for I am what's known as a 'godly' singer. I sing at funerals. Chapel or Church; Pentecostal or Congregational — I go where I'm asked. Though the Church of the Blessed Mary will always be my funeral singing home, so to speak. 'Mrs Silva has never put red to her lips, she does not smoke, or blaspheme, or take strong drink. And when she lifts up her voice, it is to sing God's praises in his house.'

Father Farrell is a nice enough man. His face is moist and white as an unbaked loaf, risen and unwrapped for the oven. His face has that unwrapped look, though his eyes are very dark and sincere. When he says his little piece, I go along with it. Shake my head, pull down the corners of my mouth in a little smile. I worry about other things like: are my new shoes too tight for my feet? Did I remember to take the price labels from the backs? Today, especially, I'm worried that the creases will start to show in my costume, which is on the small side for my ampleness. Vanity is mine.

I take my seat about half way down. *His Eye Is On The Sparrow*, I am hymn number three on the hymn-board. A few rows in the front have been left empty for the family — what family there is. Most of the people have packed themselves in at the back, with the crowds stretching out into the road. In the end, he was one of us; the local entertainer who paved the way for others — meaning Sarah Vaughan — to reach the heights.

1

I can feel the sway of bodies behind me, hear their breathing, sense the awful hush of excitement. It's the one thing I don't like about funerals today, this excitement over death, the leaning in on grief, and they won't hold back.

I'm getting too emotional; but I knew Dooley Wilson before he *was* Dooley Wilson, when he had a room in my father's boarding house just after the war. He was known as Archibald something or other then and he played piano, wonderful piano, in between features at the Bug-house or up at the young people's club — the Rainbow Club, on the bridge. All the popular tunes of the day, whatever you cared to ask for, he'd oblige. And he could imitate all the stars, with that wonderful singing voice of his. '*I'm the sheik, of Ar-ooby!*' Wonderful voice, wonderful smile. We all admired him, especially us girls.

He was a smart looking man. Big built, but smart looking, with a beautiful razor moustache, and a fine blue suit which he always wore on Sundays, when he played piano in our front parlour, with the family gathered round. Old fashioned songs like *No, John, No* or quiet hymns and spirituals — *Ezekiel Saw The Wheel*; *There Is A Balm In Gilead* — songs which pleased my father and mother especially.

I sang along with the others, but I liked to watch him play. His wide dark hands had pretty fingernails that shone like pearly shells as they struck the keyboard. He used pomade on his hair too, which he kept in a green jar by his bedside, along with a flat-backed hair-brush and four or five lavender coloured tablets of toilet soap. His room had its own, specially scented smell. We used to argue amongst ourselves, one girl and two boys, for the privilege of cleaning it out on a Saturday — as I've said, we all admired him, but from a distance — I was only a young girl then, and he was a grown man, almost a god in my young, fifteen-year-old eyes.

It was enough for me to lean my mop and bucket upside the chest of drawers and run my fingers over the things that were left on top: the hair-brush, with its smooth wooden back; the green fluted jar; the leather manicure case that opened out to show all the silvery blades and things he kept inside, all inlaid with mother of pearl, and strange and beautiful to me, as I held them in my hands.

When he changed his name to Dooley Wilson it was a shock. We'd never heard of anyone changing their name before. Our silence around the supper table made him laugh; and my father, who was a member of the Abyssinian Brethren, said something about the leopard not changing his spots; the Ethiopian, his skin. But that just made him laugh all the more, pleasantly, because he was a same island man, like my father. Still, he threw back his head and laughed, so that the shirt button came undone at his throat; and I remember how his collar opened up around his wide dark neck, like the white wings of a bird.

After that he became Dooley Wilson. You must remember him — the coloured fellow in the white suit. The one who rolls his eyes when he plays piano in that famous film and sings that famous song, so doleful! As if he already knew, even as he was singing it, poor dab, that he was destined to be forgotten. Except in our dockland part of the city.

You needed an American sounding name in those days, to help with the bookings. And I think it made him laugh, the man lying down there in the coffin; stepping into someone else's shoes and trying to make them fit. Especially as he was a different type of coloured man altogether really — our Dooley was broader, taller, darker — much darker than the light-skinned chap in the film; and with a much sweeter singing voice. Not that anyone seemed to notice; and after a while, I don't think he noticed himself. His act fell into more of a comic routine in the end, and that kept him popular in all the local clubs, long after the days with Sarah Vaughan.

Close my eyes and I can see him now. I saw him once, on my birthday, a couple of years ago. A big fleshy man, decked out in a white, satiny suit. A real professional, flashing his teeth in a smile while his fingers plinked out tunes on the piano: 'you must

3

remember this'. And this — then he'd go into his act, putting on all the voices, pulling faces:

'Dat boy over der, what's his name?'

'That boy? Why that's Sam, Miss Ilsa. Sam.'

'Dey sho' is goan be trouble, Mister Rick... '

'Play it, Sam! Sing it, Sam!'

'Please keep away from him Miss Ilsa; you bad luck to 'im!'

The voice was all honey and molasses as he rolled his eyes, and drooped his mouth to make us laugh. Under the spot-lights, his black skin had a silky looking sheen to it, still. Like black taffeta, cool, under the spot-lights. Of course, I stayed at the back with the girls from work; I didn't come forward at the end, to introduce myself. From that distance his eyes looked dull and small, like two black dots on a pair of dice...

Though what I was remembering was the time he stopped playing the piano in our front parlour and told me I had a voice. *Drink To Me Only With Thine Eyes* I sang, staring at the flowers inside the glass dome on the side-board, then at the black iron archway of the fire-place, with the blue piece of sugar paper folded inside, because it was Sunday. It was cold in the room, but the paper seemed to blaze blue when he said that: 'Gracie girl, you've gotta nice voice!'

He had tossed me that compliment like a flower, and I kept it for a long time, close to my heart.

Once I start remembering, I can't control things. The memories spin around in my head like a big roulette wheel. Black and red, blue and gold, and I can't control them. I never know when the wheel is going to stop — it drives my old man Frank to distraction.

'Sweetness, don't you go sorrowing for that man. It will only upset you, and for what?'

I was standing in front of the old fashioned mirror that hangs over our mantelpiece when Frank said that. I didn't say anything, just moved my hand along the mantel, searching for the tortoiseshell combs to put in my hair, as if I'd forgotten where I'd left them, or hadn't heard him right. But I could see his eyes,

4

looking at me through the mirror. They've got the same sort of gleam as the television set he sits in front of, my Frank's eyes. That greenish-grey sort of gleam, when it hasn't been switched on yet.

After a minute or two, when he saw there wasn't going to be an argument, he picked up the newspaper on his lap, and turned to the horse-racing. Frank knows full well I cry at funerals, I always cry a little bit, no matter whose it is. But he's jealous, Frank. He's gotten jealous in his old age. I know how it is with him, that's why I never bother saying much. Except I remembered to ask him what he was having for his tea before I went through the door. He looked up and yawned like a baby, both cheeks bellied out, bright as a brass tea-pot. But the inside, I thought, corroded. Green.

'Oh don't you worry about me,' he said. 'I'll fry up the fish.'

I had taken the fish out of the fridge earlier. Cleaned them myself, because he says the market girls don't clean them properly. I don't like cleaning them, but I did it. I took the knife with the long shiny blade, and slit open the soft, silvery under-belly, scraping out the wraggle of guts. The blood spilled dark red, like wine, and the fish felt like something carved under my hand. I cut the head off, slicing behind the fins. I was concentrating on how pretty the fish scales looked towards the tail end; they had a pearly sheen on them where they caught the light. The fin opened out, shadowy like a bird-wing, when I picked it up between my fingers and threw the head to next-door's cats.

'Are you sure now?' I had to ask, about the tea.

'Sure I'm sure. You go on and bury the dead.'

He looked at me then, and showed his teeth, brown between the ivory, in a smile. 'We've all got fish to fry, haven't we?'

'You come with me then,' I said, as nicely as I could. 'Just to show your face. Frank?'

But he wouldn't budge. So I left him there, sat in front of the television set, waiting for the two o'clock at Sandown. Yet something touched my heart to see him sat, upright, with a hand on each knee of his dark, pin-striped trousers. The trousers from what used to be his best suit, thirty years ago. And I noticed how the hair on his head was like cigarette ash; white and grey and soft as cigarette ash to the touch. Because I had to rest my hand on his head for a moment, before I went through the door.

My thoughts spin round. If the girls on my section could see my eyes fill up, they wouldn't know me.

At work I keep my head down and just get on with it. I'm a roller in the cigar factory. I cut tobacco leaf on the machines. I'm a skilled machinist, cutting the leaf on the metal die as the drum turns round. The drum is as big as a silver wheel, with twenty-four clefts cut into it. Each cleft is filled with tobacco that has been wrapped once by the girl at the other end. My leaf is the second wrapping, the one that shows.

The wheel of the drum turns round and round. The clamp picks up the cigars ... *picks up the cigars* and places them in the clefts, on and on. The finished cigars roll down the belt, and I pick them up, five at a time; scoop them up with my free hand, and stack them, row upon row in the tins, without stopping ... *without stopping*. None of that stopping and starting. Not for me. It's very rare for me to have to take my foot off the pedal. Very rare. Five hundred cigars per tin, ten tins to reach my target — that's five thousand cigars minimum — and then move on to bonus. And always cutting my leaf to get my number out.

I've been rolling cigars for years, though these days I'm on part-time. It's a well enough paid job, part-time. There's nothing romantic, or exotic, or *steamy* about it, except in other people's imaginations, other people's bad minds, as Frank would say. Sometimes, during the summer months, when it gets really hot — when the machines are roaring and the generator's going full blast — the girls will ask me to give them the lead in a song. 'Grace, give us a song, they'll say. Please!' And I'll often come out with a Christmas carol. Christmas carols have a cooling effect when you're singing them in August... and you're stuck there, in a forest of palm-green overalls, trying to cut your leaf to get your number out.

6

When I was a young girl, I sang different songs — *I Don't Want to Set The World on Fire!*; that was one of our favourites, I laugh when I think of it now. We formed a group; me, Baby Cleo and Sarah Vaughan. And practised singing in work time. Our first and last performance was at the Rainbow Club, one Bonfire night. Those two hoofing across the stage, doing the high stepping and the 'Whoo-ooh-whoo-oohs' behind me, while I stood still and sang, happy not to have to shake too much, because of my bulk. The three of us wore wrap-over pinnies, yellowy white, and brown berets. We called ourselves 'The Matchstick Girls'.

Dooley Wilson played piano for everyone who was performing. *Bye-bye Black Bird*: that was our encore! It was me and Baby who had the idea for it, then we had to have Sarah in to make the number up.

Hark at me, sat inside this darkened Church with my mind wandering. But that's always the way with funerals, I find. The emotion comes and goes, like God's grace, or the light falling in on us now, from the high windows. It comes and goes. Walking down the road towards the Church, the sun was shining where a minute before, it had been raining. Warm spring rain. Standing by the kerb, waiting to cross, I saw white cloud and blue sky mirrored in the black water as it ran into the gutter. So clear, it made me think — to see the sky beneath my feet as if the earth had gone.

There were quite a few mourners waiting outside the Church. I counted more women than men, standing under the trees in silent clumps of black. The wreaths had been propped against the funeral car windows. I saw two red hearts and a cross made up of curling, wax-white petals, and I wondered who had sent them, these tokens of love and tribulation, love and trouble.

Baby Cleo came over to talk to me. Old friends, we stood by the black-speared railings and talked a little bit. She said she'd heard a rumour that Sarah Vaughan had managed to telephone Dooley Wilson long distance, just the night before he died. Baby couldn't get over it. 'Imagine,' she kept saying, as we walked through the gate and into the Church yard. 'After all them years, oh God love 'em.' She dabbed her eyes with a hanky.

It's like a film, I thought. But I didn't say anything. People see life down here like a film.

But it's different for Baby. She was one of the girls who joined the dance-troupe, the one Dooley Wilson got together and toured the Valleys with, in the early fifties. 'Jolson's Jelly Babes' or some such nonsense they were called, and Sarah Vaughan made her name in it, blacking her face up and acting comical at the end of the line. If Al Johnson'd had an illegitimate daughter, the paper said, she'd have been it. Baby was one of the girls who came back on the charabanc, while Miss Sassy Vaughan ended up in a London show, swaying in front of a coconut tree, under a pale yellow moon. Sarah Vaughan, the coloured young lady with the Welsh name: 'The Sepia, Celtic Siren,' they billed her as. That was her gimmick: batting her eye-lashes and telling reporters she was a native, of Cardiff. They had thought she was American, but she didn't have that good a voice.

I was glad not to have been a part of the Valleys tour; the other girls were all a bit downcast when they got off the bus. Proud, but downcast.

I was surprised to see more people crowded around the side entrance as we approached. But Baby said they were waiting there just in case Sarah Vaughan were to turn up. It had said over the local radio that she wouldn't, couldn't; but people still hoped she might appear, unannounced, the way stars do.

He will always be remembered as the man who discovered Sarah Vaughan. That will be his epitaph, discovering her. Like finding something valuable and precious that no-one else had ever realised was there before. Mr Columbus.

There's only a month between our birth signs, mine and Sarah Vaughan's. Not that I believe in that sort of thing, but it makes you wonder. We both started out over the cigar factory on the same day; bunching and rolling tobacco leaf on the same machine, getting our numbers out — and singing together, high over the noise of the machinery... all those years ago. We were friends, I suppose. But it wasn't all cosy and sentimental. Oh no, because I was the roller and she was only the buncher. And she didn't like that, because I got paid more. I did more too; but you could never reason with her.

Stuff it, I wanna go home!
Stuff it, I wanna go,
But they woan let me go,
Stuff it, I wanna go home!

Except that she used to mouth *f— it*, staring down the length of our machine, Number 28, with cheek and daring in her eyes, I used to think, as I scooped up the cigars and stacked them neatly. Always the calm and steady one. Steady and responsible, that was me. And I think it used to provoke her, Sarah, into behaving worse. She was a wild one, one of those girls who wouldn't take a telling, not from the foreman, the supervisor or anyone.

'Keep your eyes off Norman, he's mine!' she was always threatening people. Or, 'Think I'm gonna spend the rest of my life in this place? Uh. Uh. Not me! So what if they pays better than the brush factory or the box factory, so what!' And that was to the foreman. She didn't care, Sarah. Most of the other girls admired her for the way she acted. But I could see it for the put on it was. She hadn't been brought up properly. Her father had left her mother with three small kids, and they were dragged up, not brought up like the rest of us. She wasn't sure about a lot of things: behind the loudness you could see. It was easy to get to her, if you put your mind to it.

Some things she had going for her — she had a good figure, with a jutting bosom and a narrow waist. And she wore her brownish gold hair swept over to one side, in imitation of some Hollywood film star or other — it used to curtain half her face, like the webbing on the mouth of a wireless, unravelled. Sometimes she tied it back, and I thought that looked much

9

nicer, neater. Not that you could tell her anything, though. Sarah Vaughan. She took that name, Vaughan, from the man her mother was living with at the time. Her real name was more common: Jones. Everybody knew that. But; her eyes were brown like toffee, and her skin was bright like tin; and if she wanted to call herself after her mother's fancy man, then she would.

The name change business came after the performance at the Rainbow Club. At first, she hadn't wanted to waste a Saturday night at home in the dockland. 'The Rainbow Club!' she said when I asked her to make up our number. She curled her lip. 'Run Off Young Girls, Boys In View — it's run by the friggin' missionaries, ain' it?' She wanted to go to the American Base in Brize Norton, where the G.I. soldiers were. But her mother said no, for a wonder. So she ended up with us, performing with me and Baby down the club, because it was some kind of a 'do' and she knew the songs, we'd sung them in work often enough, and the steps were easy.

It was raining that Bonfire Night. Everything was gleaming black with rain. And I can remember Sarah standing at the end of the bridge just in front of the club, frightened to go inside on her own. The tweed coat she had on was water-logged and rucked up at the back, and she'd straightened her hair too much in the front, greased it so that the drops of water stayed in her hair and glittered like small glass beads. That's what I remember: and the rain, the sound of it running into the gutters and flowing under the bridge as we walked up to her. And the child's voice, reciting through the club's open door, 'Tiger, tiger, burnin' bright, inna forest of the night...'

On the Monday morning she was late for work.

'A grown man, right? Wants to go out with me.'

All five of us sitting around the canteen table looked at her.

'What would he want with someone like you then, Sair, a grown man?'

But the women on the table were nudging one another and laughing. Sarah laughed along with them, then she pushed a

10

scribble of hair away from her face and took a swig from a bottle of Tizer. 'She knows him.' She nodded in my direction, smiling. 'He's a big feller, ain' he?' She took another swig from the bottle and burped. 'An' he wears this awful blue suit I'd like to set alight to, with a match...'

The women around the table laughed, and someone said, 'Well madam, are you going to meet up with this one or not?' Sarah placed her elbows on the table and leaned forward. 'Oh, I'm definitely going! He wants to give me *breathing lessons*, doan he? Says it'll improve my singing voice, ahem!' She coughed.

They all thought that was funny, and they roared. Even Baby, though she had left the club with me, and must have been as surprised as I was. We did our encore, *Bye-bye Blackbird*, and we left. People were clapping us out, because we'd been a hit. Funny. We were supposed to be funny, but it was Sarah who had been the funny one, going cross-eyed in the background as I sang. She made them laugh, as I was singing. I had to turn round to see what they were laughing at. The piano was slow and lilting. It wasn't him, he played it right. But she made it funny pulling her beret down over her eyes and acting gormless.

I watched her wipe her mouth with the back of her hand. She hadn't said anything nice about him, only nasty. She hadn't even mentioned his piano playing, or his smile, or his beautiful razor moustache. Nothing, only smut.

'An' who'd you think you're looking at?' she asked, still smiling.

'I'm looking at you,' I said in a steady voice. 'You've got no manners, have you? Sitting there with your elbows on the table, drinking out of a bottle!'

The others were embarrassed to hear me coming out with something like that, out of the blue. Everyone stared at the Tizer bottle, mesmerised by the sudden shame of it. And Sarah's mouth opened and closed a few times, before she leaned across the table with a little screech, and dragged her fingernails down the side of my face, once.

Then she clip-clopped through the canteen doors and was gone before I'd even got to my feet. But I remember holding my hands to my breast and screaming after her: 'You tart! You tart, you!'

A storm in a tea-cup. No-one had any idea what it was all about, least of all Sarah Vaughan, who got the sack for it. One misdemeanour too many, or so they said. I was only given a warning, because I'd acted out of character, they said. I saw her later on that afternoon, at four o'clock. She was standing by the fire-bucket outside the foreman's office, waiting for her wages to be made-up. I had to walk past her. She was wearing her old tweed coat, with the rucked-up hem. She muttered something horrible as I went past. When I got to the end of the corridor, I looked round; but she had taken her compact out of her bag, and was busy putting lipstick on, pulling her mouth over her teeth, and making her lips look like dark red wings.

If I felt guilty about her getting the sack, the feeling didn't last long, because only a couple of months later she was off with him, touring the Valleys as a Jelly Babe. And the rest, as they say, is history. But not for me, my mind keeps going back to it.

I remember having to go up to his room on an errand, after the fight with Sarah. I knocked at the door, my face still smarting. I was holding the blue suit over my arm. My mother had had it cleaned and ironed for him. I was hoping he'd be out. But he was only getting ready to go out. His hands were slick with pomade, so he left the door ajar and I walked inside and draped the suit carefully over the chair. He had turned back to the mirror. The contents of the manicure case were spread out on top of the chest of drawers, all silvery and pretty, with the mother of pearl inlay along each handle. He'd been trimming his moustache, I could see that; prettifying himself.

He said something about starting up a dance-troupe. 'I want you to come with us,' he said, taking more pomade from the jar and smoothing it onto his head like green ice.

'A Jolson Jelly Babe!' He was laughing in front of the mirror. There was a white shirt on the bed, whiter that the one he had on. A tie had been placed alongside the shirt, ready for going out. The tie had a pattern of small red diamonds on it. Flashy, like a playing card, I thought.

'I'm Alabamy bound!' He waved his hands like a minstrel in front of the glass, laughing at his own reflection.

'Okay, okay, Grace.' He could see that I wasn't smiling back. He turned away from the glass and faced me.

And I remember him putting his hand to my cheek and stroking it in surprise, when he saw the marks. 'You're a nice girl,' he said, over and over again. 'A nice girl, Grace. Did you know that?' He stopped stroking my face and glanced towards the open door. Then he put his arms around my body, and drew me close to him.

I felt his head against my neck.

'Ma-mmy...' he was crooning softly, singing against my neck, 'ma-ha-ha-mmee...' Leaning into my body, and singing like Al Jolson. I could see us in the mirror. His arms around the dark width of me, his head against my neck.

And I held him to me, young as I was. I put my arms around his white shirted back and held him. His shoulder blades parted under the pressure of my hands. I felt them opening out and spreading under my hands, like the white wings of a bird. Then still holding him with one hand, I leaned towards the chest of drawers, and picked up one of the silvery blades. It was the one he used for trimming his moustache. When he tried to move away, I brought the blade up against his chest, and stepped back.

I let myself into his room after he'd left us. The blue suit was hanging up behind the door, on a wire coat hanger. I put my hand inside the pockets and drew out a card of matches. The pink had bled on the matches, so I threw them into the empty fire-grate. Looking down, I noticed his passport photo, wedged between a crack in the oil-cloth and the clawed foot of the chest of drawers.

I eased the photo out with my thumb and looked at it for a long time, but I didn't see it. The wound was only a flesh wound,

13

that made a small red diamond on his shirt, before it flowered into a button-hole and had to be bandaged up. He had packed his bags himself, moving in with Sarah Vaughan that same night. But nothing came of it. Their love affair, so called. Which didn't survive her fame, how could it?

And now he was dead.

Love is a bird, that flies where it will, that's what it says in the song. But I think we travel in flocks; different flocks, cut into by our shadowy opposites always flying the other way. And not just for love, but for life.

I tucked the tiny photograph inside the wooden frame of the mirror. I remember doing that then stepping back, further and further into the darkness of the room, until it looked as though his face had been imprinted on my forehead. His eyes were just gashes of black: with dots of light at the centres, like domino pieces. Then the photograph came unstuck and dropped to the floor.

The Lord is my shepherd, I shall not want.

Father Farrell bares his teeth in a pearly-gated smile. A signal, but when I get up to sing, I find that my heart isn't in it. My face is as dry as tobacco leaf, and my lungs feel shadowy and empty like the branches of a tree in wintertime. I picture my lungs like that; and yet. And yet... as soon as the organist pumps out those opening chords... I shift my bulk and sing.

'*And I sing because I'm happ-ee, and I sing because I'm free!*' Vanity, I think, as I sense the congregation perk up behind me. All is vanity. But Baby Cleo is smiling, smiling and crying at the same time; and myself?

I have hoarded my tears like a jewel thief, but one or two steal down my face now, as I look toward the coffin for the last time. Sing! I think, even as my voice veers out of control, and *cr-a-ck-s*...

14

MICHAEL MILES HAS TEETH LIKE A BROKEN-DOWN PICKET FENCE

It was November. The girl looked up at the cloudy sky and sighed like a housewife disappointed in the whiteness of her wash. Mine looks grey, she thought, using the voice of the woman on the advert as she walked along. This was what was meant by November, that time of year when all the colours had drained away by the third week and the world was left in black and white — no, monochrome, she thought, preferring that word because it had more grey in it. Not much of black or white there wasn't, when you had a look. She thought obscurely of cameras and washing machines and vacuum cleaners and fashionable clothing: they were all the same grey tones in the magazine pictures that showed them. Only the covers on the front were in colour. She expanded the word 'monochrome' until it fitted everything into it: 'monochromatic', that was the word. It fitted everything. The girl turned her head and waited to cross to the bus stop on the other side of the road.

She saw the dog as she hurried across. It was a big dog, lying under a car, just a little way down from the stop. Its front paw was curved towards the car wheel and there was a bright red stream of blood running away from its body and down the road. The girl was surprised at how bright the blood looked. A gangly police-woman in black woollen stockings was the only one standing by the car. On guard. There was no sign of the driver. The car was a van-shaped one; blue, with strips of varnished wood on it. She never knew the names of cars.

15

Once you reached the bus-stop, you had to look over your shoulder if you wanted to see the dog. Its big furry body was a soft colour, like suede, like a mountain of hush puppies. A man came out of the paper shop; he seemed to just wander over. He was carrying a galvanised bucket filled with water. The water made him list to one side as he was carrying it. The man threw the water on to the road where the blood was, and steam came up. He didn't look bothered or anything. Just doing a job. He was wearing a sludge green pull-over; and he had a fag tucked in the corner of his mouth as he threw. He went back and got a second bucket, and threw that too. She didn't think he was the driver of the car.

Then the bus came over the top of the hill and everyone shuffled forward in the queue. The girl stepped onto the platform and showed her school bus pass. Upstairs, she sat in the front seat and thought it was funny, how everyone had looked away at first, horrified. But the bus was late, ten minutes. And in the end they were all turning to stare openly over their shoulders at the dog and the car and the police-woman. Everyone's eyes got used to it and they stared, for longer and longer and longer.

The bus pulled away from the stop, and the girl hunched forward in her seat. The police-woman was still there, standing by the car with her hands behind her back. The girl glimpsed a shiny strip of pinkish red and thought it was funny, the way her eyes seemed now to pick out all the things that were red in the atmosphere — the colour red seemed to resonate.

She mentioned it to her mother that night when she got home from school. 'It was the colour red,' she said. 'It seemed to resonate.'

'Don't come home yer with your big words!' her mother said, and threw the fish-slice into the sink to make a clatter. The girl, Lesley-Ann, stood stock-still in the doorway of the kitchen. She wondered why her mother had done that. Was it because of her condition?

Her mother was wearing a blue smock over her black skirt, there was a safety-pin in the zip of the skirt, because it wouldn't

16

do up any more. The girl knew her mother was expecting. No-one had mentioned it to her, Lesley-Ann, specifically. They would be too embarrassed: her mother and father never talked about things like that – her mother wouldn't even *say* the word 'bra' – she wrote it down when she sent Lesley-Ann to the shops. In real writing, she wrote: 'One pr. of brassiers' and, in brackets, '(36c)'. When Lesley-Ann had been about eleven (she was thirteen now) the girl behind the counter hadn't read the note properly and had sent Lesley-Ann home with a pair of boy's braces. Her mother had turned the braces over and over in her hands, fingering the silver clip-on things as if she couldn't make out what they were. 'I don't know how they come to —' she had said, and stopped. 'They're —'. She had stopped again, annoyed and embarrassed. So when Lesley-Ann came downstairs one morning and saw her mother standing at the sink in a smock she thought: oh, she must be expecting, but she hadn't said anything.

Her mother reached into the sink and picked up the fish slice. She ran it under the tap and wiped it clean with a cloth. More work! Then she gave the chips in the pan a shake. Lesley-Ann's mother shook the long handle on the frying pan as if it was someone's throat. A loud sizzling noise filled the small kitchen. Her mother looked over her shoulder at Lesley-Ann. 'Open that tin of beans for me,' she said. 'See if you can do that.'

Her father came home from work at six o'clock and they had their dinner then. They sat in the living-room and ate from the trays in their laps. The television was on in the corner. Their heads went down, then up, as the pictures flickered from light to dark on the screen. They were watching the news. Usually no-one spoke until after the news was finished. Lesley-Ann ate her sausages, beans and chips, and looked at the television-set.

In black and white, she thought, the news is. But it was grey really, when you looked at it — when you put your eyes up close to the set, you saw a swarm of grey things crawling behind the glass like millions of amoebas.

17

She thought back to the morning, when she had looked out of the window of the bus. The bus had gone past the pub, just a little way down from where the dog was, and she had looked out and seen these three people, getting into a car: two bandsmen in bright red jackets, and a girl, standing between them. The girl was wearing a mohair dress. The dress was red, but not bright red, like the men's jackets.

Lesley-Ann looked at her parents. It was on the tip of her tongue to tell them. She looked at her mother. Her mother was in a better mood, now that all the cooking was over. Lesley-Ann took a deep breath: 'Can people get married on a Friday,' she asked, 'or not?'

Her voice came out sounding like a ten-year old's. It was the type of question a ten-year old would ask, and she was given an answer straight away. Quick as a quiz contestant her mother said 'Yes, of course they can. Think there's only one day of the week people can get married on?' She looked towards Lesley-Ann's father and laughed. Her father nodded and said yes. 'Any day of the week, bar a Monday,' he screwed up his face, 'and a Sunday.'

Lesley-Ann said 'Oh,' and thought a little bit. 'They must have been going to a wedding then,' she said out loud, as if she was talking to herself. And when her mother asked her, 'Who?' Lesley-Ann said: 'These three people I saw this morning'; and she told them about the girl and the two bandsmen. 'They were all dressed up,' she told them, 'in red uniforms, the men were...'

'I wonder if that's that Kelvin.' Her mother turned to her father. He looked at her and said: 'What Kelvin?'

'You know the one I mean.' Lesley-Ann's mother knit her eyebrows together, thinking. 'You know —' She nudged his arm and said, 'You do!' He remembered then. His face cleared all of a sudden and he slapped his hand on the knee of his dungarees. 'Oh yeah,' he said, looking up at the light-bulb, 'him!'

Only a few words. Lesley-Ann stood at the stainless steel sink and dipped the plates into the hot soapy water, one by one. Her mother and father used only a few words between them, she thought, lifting a plate from out of the water and examining the bubbles minutely — but those few words spoke volumes.

Her eyes focused on the bubbles' shimmering plaid of pinks and greens and violets, before she dipped the plate back into the water and out again, hardly touching it. Just holding with four fingers, two on either side of the scalloped edges, which was how the woman did the dishes on the advert. She put the plate in the rack to drain, and went on with her thinking, trawling beneath the surface of the water for things to lift up to the light and stack. People spoke words from their mouths, she reasoned slowly. They sent them out into space, which was volume, which was air — cubic metres of air into which people sent out words — only a few at a time. And other people who were on the same wave length picked up those words and amplified them, sending out words of their own. Which became a conversation, loud and clear.

Her parents had had a conversation, about Kelvin who had gone and joined the army for ten years. And Lesley-Ann had felt she was learning something, hearing them speak. Hearing the words go back and forth as they sat there, facing the television set. Looking at, but not watching what was on the screen as they spoke to each other: ten years!... the bloody fool! You can't stop 'em — you can't... Not when they gets to a certain age... nope. They'll go their own way — well... there you are. They were almost always in agreement. Nearly always.

Lesley-Ann wondered if that meant they were made for each other, her mother and father? Made for each other; she pictured it in her mind: it was like components being made in a factory; and her parents were two halves of the same component, fitting together and working well. She, Lesley-Ann, was the odd one out. She felt it suddenly.

And what about this new baby? Lesley-Ann moved away from the sink and lifted the chip pan from the stove. She dismissed the new baby from her mind. It was never spoken of, at least, not in her hearing. Except that she did hear things, relayed over

19

cups of tea to the neighbours, the women, when they came to congratulate. Still-born, she heard. Breech. And once, when the radio played a song about a baby coming down to earth at Christmas, her mother had shouted: 'Out that!'

The fat had set in the frying pan, white and smooth, and slippery as snow inside the round black rim. She held the handle almost upright and gazed into the whiteness of the pan, as if she was gazing at a blank wall.

'You out here to play around or what?'

Her father had his hand on the closet door, ready to pull it open and remove his mac. He was going down the off-licence. He went down there every Friday, as soon as he had gone over his wage slip with her mother. The wage slip was a long ribbon of paper which they held between them. It was coloured pink and had faint blue numbers on it: deductions (look!), stoppages. Her father always came back from the off-licence with two packets of crisps for each of them, a bottle of cider and a small bottle of pop for Lesley-Ann. It was like a celebration, every Friday night.

She picked up the fish-slice and began to shovel industriously. The cold fat slid off the metal tines and into the pedal-bin like curls of slush. When she raised her head, her father had gone.

Rom-pom-pom-pom-pom-pom-pom! From London we invite you to... rom-pom-pom-pom-pom-pom-pom!

It was nearly half-past seven. Lesley-Ann crunched her crisps and drank her pop in front of the telly. She was sitting on the pouffe with her knees up and her back against the knubbly moquette of the settee. Her parents were sat one at either end of the settee, with herself on the pouffe in between. The pouffe was made of small, black and white squares of imitation leather, and Lesley-Ann felt like Little Miss Muffet sitting on it. She felt herself shrinking in size as she sat there.

Like a small child, she gazed up at the walls and the ceiling. The room was bright and cosy now, with the curtains drawn. The shaded light bulb deepened the colouring on the walls to a buttermilk yellow. She could see the swirl of the brush marks in the distemper when she looked straight up. And the room was hot. Her father had banked up the fire with small coal when he came in. Now the small coal glowed dull red in the fire basket like a heap of cola cubes dusted with sugar, which was the ash.

The man on the television said: *Take Your Pick! And here is your host, your quiz 'n' quizzer — Michael Miles!* Then the audience clapped, and while they were clapping, Lesley Ann's father rustled the paper and spoke behind it. 'There's a cowboy film on eight o'clock,' he said. 'After this.' He lowered the paper and stared at the television set.

'Oh you and your cowboys!' said Lesley-Ann's mother. 'That's all you minds. Cowboys!'

'It's a good film.' Lesley-Ann's father spoke without turning his head away from the set. 'You'll like it,' he said. 'There's Mexicans in it.'

Lesley-Ann listened while her mother told her father he always said that, just to get her to watch the rubbish. Her father knew her mother hated the cowboys, she thought. Except if there were Mexicans — they always played guitars and sang, so she didn't mind them so much. *Larame, Lone Ranger, Wagon Train, Wyatt Earp, Sugar Foot, Maverick, Whip-lash, Raw-hide, Bonanza* — she listed all the cowboy programmes in her head as the picture went funny on the television screen, and her mother got up to fix it.

'Let's try it on number five.' Her mother pressed the white plastic button on the dial, and the dial went round like a fire cracker and stopped at number five. But the picture there was worse, so she moved the aerial. The aerial was a big wire hoop with a brown plastic pad on the bottom of it. Slowly, slowly, her mother moved the aerial along the polished wood. Like a hand moving a glass on a ouija board, she called up voices.

But no pictures, only zig-zag lines. There was a burst of clapping — there! Then the picture steadied itself. 'There — you've got it!'

'Have I?' Her mother stepped away from the television-set,

21

watching the screen all the time. The picture went again; oh! only this time a word came up, and they read it slowly: *Newsflash*.

Lesley-Ann had never seen a newsflash before, but her mother said, 'Hey, newsflash!' so she knew it must be something important and listened carefully. There were two in the space of ten minutes. The first newsflash said the President of the United States had been shot. The second one said he was dead. 'We regret to announce...' There were no pictures. Only a man sitting at a desk in front of a curtain both times.

Lesley-Ann got up from the pouffe and sat on the couch to rest her legs. She measured the distance between herself and her mother and father as she sat in the middle. None of them spoke, but they watched what came on the television. There was no more *Take Your Pick* and at the back of her mind, Lesley-Ann imagined the procession of contestants, going on with the game without them watching. Instead there was more news. And at the end of the news, they showed a photograph of the President that filled the whole screen. Then they played a slow march, and a pair of curtains were drawn across his craggy light-grey smiling face, until there was nothing left to see. That showed he was really dead, thought Lesley-Ann, when the curtains came across and shut him off like that. The music ended and the announcer said that they were closing down now, BBC and ITV, as a mark of respect.

'Well, you might as well out that now,' said Lesley-Ann's mother. The awful music had started up again. 'There's nothing else on, the man's just said.' They looked at the clock. It was still quite early, but after a moment, Lesley-Ann's father walked over to the television-set and clicked the switch off, then he bent down and pulled the plug out. Her mother raked what was left of the fire with the poker and asked Lesley-Ann to bring her the teapot from the kitchen.

Then, her mother stood by the grate, one hand on the small of her back as if she was tired, and poured. A terrible hissing noise rose up from the cinders, and specks of ash flew from the fireplace and around the room. Lesley-Ann flailed her arms in front of her face like a wild thing, fighting off the ash, but her parents stood quite calmly, waiting for the air to clear.

IN VERY PLEASANT
SURROUNDINGS

I

Open your mouth sometimes, she said to Reynolds. And make out like you're talking. Otherwise they says: *there's quiet, y'ruzzbandiz* — her voice went up, mimicking the other women patients' inquisitiveness.

Reynolds stood by the locker. As usual he was quiet and awkward; unassuming.

What shoes you got on, uh?

We all peeked over the bed as Reynolds shuffled uncomfortably. His shoes were thick white leather brogues; good quality, but white.

White! I knew it, Barbara said, and her voice sounded sick with triumph. I knew it! Bloody wedding shoes he've got on, she said. The stupid — her lips went thin and she closed her eyes. Just to show me up the stupid — her eyelids were dark with pain.

We laughed, the rest of us around the bed. Laughed out loud, enjoying the joke. This was exactly the same as at Connor and Cristin's engagement party. Reynolds had worn the same shoes then, and Barbara had jumped up and hissed in his ear: everybody else dressed smart and you turn up in bloody baseball daps ya stupid bloody bleeder you, ya. Reynolds had smiled his soft smile and asked her to dance. They had danced. Barbara loved to dance, no matter what. She was a good dancer. The other guests watched them mash-potato, turkey-trot and do the dog. They clapped when they sat back down.

I clapped too, proud to be her friend and next-door neighbour.

She seemed so full of life, Barbara, none of the people there realised she was Connor's mother. She was only forty-three. Connor himself wasn't so happy, though. I saw his face over Cristin's shoulder as they shuffled past. He was staring hard.

All I needs is the music me! Barbara had said and laughed, whew! fanning her face with a cardboard plate, whew!

D'you want to go again? Reynolds had held out his small fat hand, chocolate brown with the bright gold cluster on the littlest finger. Come on, I knows you do, he said. Come on — he pulled on her arm, but half-way up from her seat she'd turned on him. Oh no you don't, she said. You don't get me up again you don't. Her voice went high and accusatory: I know what you're out to do. You're out to put me in my box, ain' you? she said, and sat back down on the floral corner suite for the rest of the night.

She was careful of her heart. The doctor had warned her about high blood pressure, and the weight she was carrying, and the pressure on her heart, the danger of a fatal heart attack. She had it to go all that summer — it was a running joke when she told anyone throughout that summer. Doctor Fischer said, *Mrs Cruz you could go, shwuump! just like that*, she said to Connor. What with my weight and everything. We'll have to get you on that day trip to London then, said Connor, before you do go.

How's the blood pressure now? I ask, reminded of that time.

Still there, she shrugs, impatient, weary.

And how long've you had it?

Years. It is three years, I count on three fingers as her eyes look fearfully past me to the nurse outside. But high blood pressure is not the problem anymore, we all know that. Silence, except for a tiny clicking noise in the corner. I look across: Reynolds standing next to the locker, nervously clicking his false teeth. His dentures are wedged in, white as a block of chewing-gum along the upper side of his mouth. Click, and again the tiny click. The rest of his teeth are yellow, saffron yellow.

Barbara's mother Bernadine breaks the silence. Here we are, all of you — chocolates! She creaks up from her winged chair by

25

the bed and offers round the box. Go on, take one! She forces everyone to take a chocolate, except for Barbara, and Reynolds, who holds his hand in front of his face and shakes his heavy head regretfully. Not for me thanks, not for me. You on a diet? Bernadine chuckles as she returns to her seat and parks herself down heavily, spreading her fur-trimmed coat. She is seventy-five years old and not as sprightly as she used to be. Ooh, these are nice! Bernadine looks at all our faces for confirmation: nice? And we give it, happily, thankfully. Nice, yes.

I'm not to do no housework! Barbara says this in a rush, staring up at our chewing mouths, like a child, lost. Only a bit of hoovering, she says finally, looking at Connor first; then at Cristin... perhaps. Mmmn, our heads are nodding down at her as we chew, steadily, rhythmically, mmmn.

I'm to do nothing that could destroy the treatment, Barbara says, and stops. Her eyes are empty as she searches through her mind for another phrase, then latches onto it like a great truth: I've got to think positive! she says. I've got to fight!

'Course you've got to fight, says Connor. He unwraps another chocolate from the box, pops it into his mouth. Can't win nothing in life unless you fight. He chews, noisily.

Barbara has been diagnosed as having cancer. After a week of tests and two months of uncertainty, the answer has come through: cancer. Not fibroids, like Dr Fischer said it was. No simple D&C. That was just to get me into hospital, says Barbara. But I knew it was cancer, all along I knew! she smiles and shakes her head. Triumphant for this one small moment, because she's been proved right.

I look round for a stool as she starts talking about her radium treatment: the radium. Ten minute sessions. All the stools are taken. I turn back to the bed. The radium... that's to kill it off snap! she says, snapping her thumb and index finger together smartly to make the sound. We watch as she draws a hand across her stomach, shows us where the gold seeds will be sewn, inside the stomach a line of gold seeds. That's to — *counteract* the

26

radium. She says this slowly, carefully, then looks at us. Bernadine makes a grab at Barbara's abdomen, clutching up a heap of bedclothes. Someone'll run off with her, she chuckles. Once she've had gold seeds put in.

There's a small blue plastic madonna attached to the metal frame of the bed. What's this! I say laughing, pointing.

St. Vincent de Paul's left me that, last night. Barbara turns her head. That's holy water inside there, she says, from Lourdes. Everyone looks at the little statue. The water inside it seems blue, because of the cheap blue plastic.

I'm going to Lourdes when I gets out of hospital. Barbara scans our faces with her tired eyes. I'm going to work for the sick — don't laugh! Don't mock — she smoothes the counterpane with her free hand (the other hand has a tube stuck in it, attached to the drip) and carries on talking. Dreamy voiced, as though she's talking to herself: three o'clock this morning I was wide awake, staring out that window... When she says this, the rest of us glance over our shoulders. Involuntarily, we find ourselves peering into the night, which is royal blue behind the glass, with just a few sodium lights, orange in the distance... Barbara's voice reclaims our attention:

I took it, what he had to tell me, that Consultant. I took it —

You took it like a man! says Connor, butting in. Putting his close-cropped head towards the bed, and butting in. His mother's face looks up at him, stunned when he says this. But five minutes later, she raises her right arm: And I took it — she hooks her right arm into the air and looks at all of us. Like a man! she says and laughs, as we catch on and laugh, quite loudly.

II

Here is the place. From across the bay it's a bluff, blue headland rising up and jutting out from the sea. It is called Atterton. In a previous life, at night, from my block of flats, high-rise, my eyes have picked out the fluorescent orange lights, bobbing around in the blueness which is the sea, I fathom, at night, from across the bay.

I am a camera. I was. No sound. But now I am here, in Atterton, and the bone-white, round-white hospital clock, tick ticks on the wall. Bone-bright and white as the moon through the cubicle curtains. I shutter my eyes. The nurses say sleep. Close your eyes, an injunction. Close them, they say. Sleep. You must sleep. But I am a camera. And this hospital is like a hotel by the sea. It overlooks the sea, which beats outside the plate-glass windows of my mind. Incessantly. The sea. My mind, this ocean. Fast, rewind.

Yesterday, it was. It must be yesterday by now, the nurse told me that a mad scientist wanted to blow up the moon. Blow up the moon? I cried, looking up at her face, looking down at my arm as she probed with the needle. My transfusion? Why? I asked her. And why, politely, would they want to do that? Hold still. She'd heard it on satellite that morning, she said. Hold still! as the needle slid in and she straightened herself up to adjust the clear tubing. And above her head, the crackling red, plastic red packet of blood. The metal stand jangled.

Over three minutes! There's veins like old tyres! she said. She turned her head to laugh. Her fingers chip white, straight-cut, fingers on ketchup. Adjusting the flow. She looked at her watch and said, Scientists! Remembering, scientists, they're as mad as hatters, aren't they Mrs?

Nurse?

Tongue untied, I opened my mouth to ask her, I said: Nurse how long will this take? As I watched her watch her watch-face that was pinned to her pocket on a chain above her heart. A fob. She said, well, it's difficult to say. Exactly. Squeezing the metal rim as if the glass inside was molten, pliable. Not *too* long. And don't worry! she smiled. It's only a top up, she smiled and let it drop.

Swish swash, that dry sound in my ear rings, still. Swish swash

28

of the leaf green curtains, as the nurse was stepping through. Then thought of something — looking back, she smiled a sliver. And what about the tides, she said, the oceans! Have they thought about that? The clincher. Time and tide, she said, they wait for no man, Mrs — isn't it?

Since then I have heard the tea-trolleys roll by, nil by mouth. My throat is parched. Dry. And my eyes feel flat, like push buttons in my head. How many hours since then? Only connect, my mind says. Only connect with the tubing, and each packet's slow red oozing as it empties into my veins. This must mean, surely, that time is passing?

Slowly, slowly, the tide comes in so slowly. And here I lie, like a narrow shadowed stone. Bluish, thin-pinched, waiting to take on that *roseate* Picasso glow. Another period, but for how long? Who knows? My consultant is as cautious and inconstant as a weather-man. You cannot pin him down and I don't want to. I need that space. Hello, I'm Mr So-and-so. Hello. The held out hands are large, and filmy to the touch. Greyish white, disposable as gloves, but grafted on. Hello, I'm Mr Sew-n-sew.

And I am a camera, I told him as he smiled and passed along. Once, I lived in a high-rise block of flats where the lift went up and down like a roll of film on sprockets. Floor by floor we blinked, as the doors slid open and the light came flooding in on us. Such cell-like spaces we live our lives in; divisible and dividing, always dividing. Though at night, I lived in a lighthouse, fifteen storeys high, as the windows lit up one by one and blazed forth. Safe as houses in the darkness, safe...

My flowers are falling. Blue petals detach themselves and fall, like raffle tickets. Why do people send them? And the hospital sells post-cards in the foyer — A view of the sea, from Redcliffe Ward. My ward. The walled garden. The white chapel — simple as a Utrillo, and sold in aid of — but what do I put on them? Wish you were here?

In this Edwardian, Victorian town by the sea. The Edwardian park, set high on a hill where the green grass ripples. And

29

families sit under the red roofed rotunda, and point. The parents point, towards a widening rift of light, a dazzling silver band between the clouds. William! Alice! Mary! Look, the sea, they cry. The sea —

From the cliff-tops of my mind, I wonder: what draws us to the edge of things?

This seaside town, with its grey pebble beach and renovated pier, its esplanade lined with cafes that say *Ho*-made ice-cream sold here, is never short of visitors.

Even on sunless days you will see them shuffling forward, the crowd, pulled by some magnetic force towards that iron strutted edifice, the pier, where their dark moving figures form a frieze between sea and sky, causing you to realise, because the sun has gone in, and the sky is over-cast, that these are not sight-seers merely, but pilgrims driven to reach that far off point in the middle distance: the pier's end. And having reached it, they will lower their awkward heads and drape their many arms anemone-like over the sides, to gaze, tranced and slumberous, into the waters below.

What are they looking at, the crowd? What rivets their attention? Perhaps it is the absence of their own reflection that startles? For the sea is glazed and cold as glass. Vitreous, slow moving, mirror-like, but not, the sea bevels and bellies on its way, inviting their glances, drawing them in like a looking glass — only to bring them face to face with a cloudy grey, falling away into nothingness: the void.

From the safety of the pier, looking down, the crowd hugs the iron railings to itself, hugs the frisson of fear unto itself, then turns away, then turns away.

Aye, and there's the rub!

What shall we do? What shall we ever do?

The temperate voice reciting says: take each day as it comes. Yes? And one day at a time. Oh, and fight. Yes, you must fight. Never give up hope (because hope's a dope). Open your mouth now, wide. And take your tablet. Comfortable? We'll do our best to make you comfortable, as comfortable as we can, yes. And sleep, you must sleep.

Is that a hopeful sign? I take these signs for wonders, hard to tell, but. Focus, I must focus. These fragments have I shored against my ruin:

Gravitation (verb), the pull of — Returns me to the cliff-top where the wind gusts in my ears like the shaking out of bed-sheets; it flattens the long stemmed sea grasses that fur the cliff's edges and carries the *chink, chink, chinking* noise of the men and boys hammering below. Peering over the side through the grass, I catch a glimpse of orange waterproof, as orange as the webbing on a duck's feet. And that makes them, the men and boys, amphibious? At home on land or sea?

The sea, which from this distance appears to be a stain on the sky. If I didn't *know* that greyness was the sea, I might think it was the sky, falling away into nothingness.

Gravitation (verb), the pull of— Raindrops, which are finite in size. Ergo, the smaller you get, the bigger they seem. Therefore, the smaller you get, the more you are affected by...

What, falling drops of rain? Yes, but then, the *less* you are affected by gravity! *The unbearable lightness of being* grown suddenly bearable. Shall I float then, inside this body which has become an ark of bones? My rib-cage, feel: here are the struts of my rowing boat, already in place — and no man is an island, no, but — perhaps I need to find the right perspective? Mechanical laws of... adapt, become accustomed, acquiesce? For after all the proper end of life, is death. And I am tired... But I am a camera! No.

Behind the plate-glass window beats the sea, cold and grey and churning, churning. Once, the glass itself was molten liquid burning, burning. This sea will freeze me till I burn, like ice...

They've packed me up with ice. In my insides to stop the bleeding. Never mind the pain... am I falling unconscious? Wake up! They packs you up. Carn' give you nothin', only push — into the womb, with packs of ice. They've got to, to stop the bleeding...

31

Come on, fight! Hold on to my hand now Mama (am I hurtin your hand? I am, I'm hurtin it) and fight! Huh, uh huh. You listening?

Uh? I was standing at the basin cleaning my teeth an' I heard this *whoosh!* The nurses ran towards me shouting out: Don't move! I had my toothbrush in my hand, I thought what's happenin'? They're rushing me down on the trolley and I'm still with the toothbrush in my hand and I'm askin 'em: what's happening? I didn't know, did I? But they knew, the nurses. They ran towards me shouting out: Don't move! All that red around me. I thought it was my dressing gown had fallen. I heard this *whoosh!* So fast... and I'm looking down, there was all this — an' I thought what's all this red around my feet? Huh, uh huh. Am I dying, Connor? Am I dying? (No! you're not dying!) Because if I'm dying, doan fetch me a doctor, fetch me a priest...

III

Tonia drove Bernadine to the hospital late in the afternoon after Connor had phoned. The old lady was trembling with fear, while Tonia tried to stay calm. After all, I am not family, Tonia told herself. Only a friend, she told herself, as Bernadine sat on the back seat in her black fur coat and whimpered quietly.

They bought tissues in the shop at the hospital entrance. Tonia pulled the yellow thread on the cellophane wrapper and offered them to the old lady as though they were cigarettes. Going up in the lift, Bernadine pressed the paper hankies to her trembling mouth and gazed upwards, following the little red arrow with hypnotised eyes as it directed them upwards. The old lady's skin was netted with lines, and dotted here and there with velvety moles. Like the dots on a mourning veil already in place, Tonia thought, as the lift stopped and they tottered out onto the sixth floor, where the sign on the pastel coloured wall said Haematology.

At the far end of the corridor, they saw a man who looked like

Reynolds disappearing through the double doors. Tonia called, but he didn't hear. They had to ask an auxiliary for directions. She gestured vaguely and they crept along, peering into the glass fronted rooms and side-wards, timidly. One of the cell-like rooms had its blinds half drawn, for privacy. They went past it once, without thinking, then tip-toed back.

I've fought!

To their surprise, Barbara was sitting up in bed waiting to greet them. As soon as she sensed their shadows hovering by the door, she turned to greet them. *I've fought!* The lemon-coloured night dress she was wearing seemed bright to their eyes, like candle flame, as she turned to greet them, hardly waiting for Connor and Cristin to stop smiling and vacate their seats, before she began to speak.

MOTHER COUNTRY

When it was over they gave me a doll. A doll which was small and light-weight, but covered in the softest of mottled skins. A mottled, soft-skinned baby doll, carefully placed in the crook of my arm. There we are, the nurses exclaimed in unison. A real doll!

This said, they stood back beaming, while my head drooped in weary examination. No! I cried in a sudden panic. No! This can't be it! I looked at the nurses incredulously.

But what's the matter? Their voices were saccharine. She's a real doll! they said. A real little doll. Their simpering faces came closer. You are, aren't 'oo? they cooed. Aren't 'oo, eh?

This obtuseness, which appeared to contain an element of the deliberately wilful, irked me.

Who are you trying to fool? I asked the one standing in for the mid-wife, crossly. 'A real doll!' This, I shook my head and pointed, is not a real doll. Real dolls have short, chubby legs. Legs made out of laminated plastic; that stay up in the air when you push them up, and don't just flop, like these do. I gestured contemptuously. And another thing, I picked up one of its hands to demonstrate, the fingers and toes of a real doll are always stuck together, while these can be s-e-p-a-r-a-t-e-d out!

Tired but satisfied, I let the hand drop and laid my head back on the pillows. But just then, its tiny fingers lifted automatically and curled around the mouldings of its left ear. This caused me to hesitate — for certainly that ear, so intricately moulded and wax-like, appeared to be as unhearing as a real doll's ear. And then, as if to encourage my suspicions, one of its eyes fell open.

This lone blue eye, round and grey-blue as a stone, reminded me of something. And scarcely daring to hope, I grasped its shoulders with both my hands, and prepared to give it a shake. For that is what you must do with dolls, isn't it? When you want to make both eyes open at once? But the softness of its skin again unnerved me and I fell back on the bed, repelled.

Girl! said the doctor in expostulatory fashion the next morning, dolls are just dolls. What you have here, is a real live baby!

A baby? I pretended to chew this over, ruminatively. What are dolls meant to be then? I asked. And if they're not meant to be perfect babies, ideal in every respect, then why are we encouraged to nurse them and put them in prams and wheel them about, etcetera, etcetera?

The doctor, who had a boiled pink face and iron grey hair, compressed his lips and smiled, grimly. Here, he said, yanking the form out of the cot and placing it in my arms. Take your baby and perhaps you will begin to understand.

That was the start of my 'hands-on training', though its overall effects have been curiously minimal.

My brain is in a freezer-box inside my head. My movements are all in slow motion: detached, impersonal and incompetent. The triumph of disassociation I think, as the hospital staff elbow me aside with tut tut tuts of impatience.

Someone's gone and given you the wrong mammy!

The Irish nurse brings her face close to its face, whispering fiercely as she tugs a pair of white cotton gloves down over its claw-like hands. I follow the operation with polite indifference. Poor circulation! She stands and looks at me accusingly. They're to trap the heat, she says slowly. The cotton mittens. You'll make sure she keeps them on her little hands now, won't you?

Oi will! I cry, beaming up at her. Oi will, narse! The nurse's broad cheeked face flushes an angry red at this, but her sandy lashed eyes rest upon me, very still and calm, like greenfly. Every child is a gift from God, she hisses softly. And the sooner you learn to accept that fact, young lady, the better it will be for you, mark my words!

With that she turned on her heels and exited through the open door, leaving me to call out after her, in my clear piping voice: Oh? So this is from God, is it? Then God should be reported to the RSPCA, the dog! Going around giving people unwanted gifts! 'Have yourself / a merr-y litt-le Christ-mas!' My puckish laughter accompanies the tread of her footsteps until she reaches the comer, abandoning me to my thoughts and silence.

An hour or so later, I lie propped up on the bed, gazing at the bundle in my arms. Time for baby's lunch, they said, and placed it there. In my arms. I start to feed it its bottle, docilely enough. But as I look down, I can feel myself ballooning, up and up and up — like Glumdalclitch, an alarming sensation, this feeling. Of overwhelming power, of being bloated with power… could crush — just, use my arm like a vice and crush its head, its skull, in the crook of my arm… Or I could take it by the legs. Its legs hang down so thinly look, like the legs of a chicken, while the long soles of its feet… are very red. Very long and red — I could take it by the legs, the ankles perhaps, and dash its brains out. One swing against the wall, that far wall, where there's a clock…

I concentrate on the clock, on the clock-hands moving slowly around the clock-face, under the glass, on the far wall. In twenty minutes time, I tell myself firmly, you'll be clover. Standing in the white tiled baby kitchen, attached to the silver tea-urn, having your milk drained off. Scientifically drained off. Shrinking you down, deflating you in size, returning you to what you were — in size. I look down at the bundle in my arms and wonder, what is it? This burden?

It has learned to suck, look. Perfect lips, quite perfectly shaped. The little tongue moves against the teat of the bottle, quite strongly! Such a pretty, heart shaped mouth as it sucks, why do I do it? Why do I do, what I do?

Big push! Come on, no — take a deep breath, then lips together and push! From your bottom — no! You're blowing through your mouth. Next time it slides down we want a big push!

I got me one liddle doll, yeah? One boneca!

36

Push! the doll's head sliding down between my legs. He said: push *bébé*, push *bébé* — two headed now, I am a doll lying on a bed, in another country — a vast bed whose golden brown covering stretches wide as the Mojave which is chenille; which is a counterpane of corrugated velvety sands, of burning yellow sands wound round with red, which is red like the jam in a swiss roll. *Hey boneca!*

From the monitor, its heart-beats pound like footsteps, marching. They will march right down through my body — trample their way through, forcing a Panamanian birth-canal through the isthmus of my body.

No, I *can't* any more. It doesn't want to come — I can't help it, if it doesn't want to come —

Nonsense! It's got this far on its own, Miss! — come on, push!

I am a doll. I lie on the bed, the pampered, favoured one. The caramel-featured mulatta, with the coral red mouth that smiles so graciously. No one would imagine that I'm a *two* headed doll, that my voluminous satin skirts, edged with gold brocade and arranged so decorously, conceal another head, another doll, between my legs.

Oh *mai*? I drop my own head forward, calling out sweetly: *mai*? Hello? Are you still down there — wait, let me hoist my skirts a little higher, and scrunch right down — ola! There she is look — my African mammy! See her face, that jetty black face poking through? See her red, red mouth, and big hooped earrings? They are made of brass, naturally, while mine are made of gold. No problem. Her turban is of plain white cloth, wrapped round (while mine is a twist of gauzy blue silk, piled high with tiny oranges, a la Miz Carmen Miranda, Yo!) and her gown is a very humble one, very washed and faded. Manchester cotton is it? Imported? No, not quite, it feels more... homespun, a sort of blue, homespun twill — your eyes are glaring at me, mammy —

Don't look at me with those eyes like that — your eyes are awfully bright and glaring — like the hospital lights above my head. Round spots of light, hard as quartz in stone, bearing down

37

on me, boring in on me — Oh!... mammy... no! She has lifted her skirts of homespun blue — look, suddenly upped and lifted them, oh no! My mammy's vast blue skirts are falling... from a great height, like a blue tent falling. Ensnaring my face, shutting me off, covering my face and shutting me off, completely.

Let's see what we've got then, shall we?

(Help, help!)

The hospital sheet is falling. The nurse darting forward, lets the blue sheet fall. It covers my face like a winding sheet as I twist and turn in panic, help! In the darkness I can feel myself falling back, receding into history... A doll on a bed, upended now, who am I?

Congratulations!

My short brown legs on the bed, shiny with sweat and bent at angles, like the arms and elbows of a swimmer, with the small head in between them, poking out, thrusting through... Congratulations!

She's a real doll! A real little doll!

End so fair, said the lady German doctor, coming forward. I *kent* get over your baby's fairness, it is am-azing, *end* it's not going to change...

Know me! I whisper suddenly, fiercely, to the bundle in my arms, know me!

But her eyes offer no recognition. Like hard blue stones, they look without seeing — Know me! I drag that teat away from her mouth and wait, expectantly. I wait... Yet she continues to suck: suck, suck, suck, that heart-shaped mouth, sucking in air — and silence, sucking in the long, long, silence — until the message travels through to her brain and she puts out her hand, and cries, quite loudly.

But she puts out her hand! Amazing, for it is the touch of her hand, her baby hand, with the small white fingers stiff and cold upon the warm, brown flesh of my arm, that starts the thaw – that unfreezes my heart – drip, drip, drip. I put the teat back into her mouth, and watch her tiny fingers uncurling. Entranced, as one by one they uncurl in the warmth of my body-heat, and then wave in the air, palely, like sea-anenomes.

DIDO ELIZABETH BELLE —
A NARRATIVE OF HER LIFE (extant)

...the next day I rose up early from my bed and left my Uncle's house. I did not look behind me but struck out for the woodland path as swiftly as I could. It was a blue misty morning, one of those blue September mornings that cause the heart to quicken always, with a sense of promise. This thought buoyed my spirits and kept me steadfast on my journeying; so that it seemed but a short space of time before I reached the outermost perimeters of my Uncle's estate. Now the shady groves and pretty meandering walkways were suddenly replaced by an altogether wilder, more untutored landscape.

I gathered my skirts about me and climbed a stile. The air was cold on my face. A welcome cold I thought, after the oppressive and sweltering heats of the summer past. My clumsy wooden pattens rocked against the second most hurdle of the stile causing me to put out both my arms like a scarecrow, to save myself from falling. Balancing thus, I pondered whether Adam and Eve had gone forth from Paradise on such a morning as this? If so, then they had rather rushed towards their banishment, I reasoned, than approached it with intimations of dread. For the world before me was glorious. Glorious in the studied green and blueness of its promise. A sudden vision of my Uncle's house, that pretty white mansion of many many rooms, caused tears to start up in my eyes. It was all I had ever known of as home. Caenwood. Our family 'sweet-box' at Caenwood.

The tears stood in my eyes and grew, luminous as lenses – then astonishingly my feelings about turned once again, for all that lay before for me was now magnified perforce, through this self-same vale of tears! And I saw every leaf and berry and tangled stem of grass, separately. And every drop of dew that was upon them, brightly shining, separately. And every cobweb thread strung with beads of crystal, each one cold and shining, separately. Then I lost my balance and toppled over and I fell; and rolled; down, down, down, the steep and narrow woodland track...

It was a strange green world I fell into, it acted upon my senses strangely. High above my head, the wind stirred the leaves on the trees, blowing them this way and that; exposing their pale green undersides; and setting up a constant rustling noise that sounded in my shell-like ears, murmurous as the sea. Indeed, I began to feel as though my body had lodged itself at the very bottom of the sea. For everywhere the light was green; and of such a viscous, liquid green, that seeds and dry leaves floated down through it as sediment floats through water, slowly. A snail passed by my head. At once I was struck by the crystalline beauty of its shell; the prismatic glow of each coil; and the undulating manner of its movement — pulling the soft parts of its body over a fallen twig, as if swimming through its own slime.

Lulled, I took in a deep breath; but began almost immediately to experience the most terrifying sensations of panic; for my nostrils were filled, not with good air, but with the poisonous exhalations of the plants and rotting vegetation around me – so that rearing up, I began to thrash and struggle through the undergrowth, tearing my skin and clothing; desperate for air, life-giving air – yet conscious all the while that I was drowning. And that I *must* drown, in this strange green world where all things turned to rust; and fell like the leaves, or stayed to wither on the root, brown and skeletal as the dancing fern that brushed, brushed brushed, against my face, obscuring my vision and stifling my exhausted screams at birth.

What I remember next is the sunlit clearing.

Ho! what she remembers next is the sunlit clearing.

Dazed I stumbled into it, the patch of sunlight, and saw the man. Crouching on the far side of a steep bank. He was —

Fishin. I was.

41

I saw his heavy hands move. I saw the red inside them, lit up by the sun. They were flesh and blood. His hands, that he held before him.

Only holding out the net, I was. Trying to coax the fish.

The hair stood on his head like blades of grass. Short bladed grass, half green with sunlight. When a shape moved through the water, he crouched right down and slid his hat on quickly.

Ho, yes. I did that then, because I see'd it coming!

Swimming through the water — Yes.

The body of him was white. When he pulled his shirt off.

An' my leathern breeches I would've pulled them off an all, as clean as bark is peeled from a tree, but I stops and hauls 'em up again, no time —

Then I wades into the water — brrr! just as the fish swims into the net. The surface of the water was spangled with light, but the mesh of netting was black and cloudy, voluminous as a mourning veil, wrapped round the fish. I saw the gelid amber of its eye, the pink and tender mouth. And marked the way its body hung wet and heavy as a stone inside the net; almost inanimate. Oh werry inanimate an stone-like I'd say, apart from the blessed tail! All the energy an life was in the tail — you should have seen me struggle!

Oh yes, as she flipped and twisted, this-er-way an that.

All to no avail. A mighty upthrust and the fish was flung violently into the air. It landed in the grass, and he clambered after it, the man; wildly on all fours. His long armed body was thinly furred – with colourless hairs that glinted in the sunlight. And his hands were knobbled red. Horrified I watched as he wheeled himself around and stayed the fish's movement with a blow. Smack!

I stunned her with a rock that was lying near by. Then I whips her up by the tail an brings her head down smartly. But all on a sudden something makes me leery, an I looks up quick — an damn my eyes! If I ain't being watched —

Well I knows when I'm awake, so I wasn't dreaming. Not I,

42

when I sees her standing there. The negro-girl, sombre as a linnet, standing in the clearing all alone. Feet brown an naked, clogs held in her hands. What's this thinks I, with a grin. A child o' nature, roamin through the woods and meader-lands at will? But that were passing strange, that were. To see a negro-girl in a woodland glade. Passin. An it set my mind to wondering as I tries my luck — Hey my honey, hey! For I'm a ketcher by trade, I am. I ketches snakes 'n sparrers, badgers and hedge-hogs. Warmints, water-beetles an such like. Fish. Though snakes is my speciality. George Augustus Hercules Adams. Showman 'n ketcher to the King and Queen respective, I am.

My honey. My sugar. My sweet. This lowly man, the author and disposer of my fate? He stands beside the waters and he calls me. *Chirrup-eek, eek eek eek gweek. Chirrup-eek!* As if I were a wild thing in the woods. He calls me. But I do not move. Four-handed leaves blow past my feet as he advances — I see the whole of his person now. But still I do not move. Dry leaves decorate the grass with scrolls of bronze, as on a carpet; and fallen among them are the berries, glazed dark red. And the acorns too, fallen from the trees and strewn — the seeds of things, the shells of things, all strewn before his feet as he advances.

Have you runned away? I asks the creature softly. For I'm talkin all the time I'm a-walkin up to her. Have you gone and left your Master, hev you? Or your Mistress, perhaps, says I with a glance at her finery. Gown, apron, petticoats, they was all in tatters to be sure. But damn my eyes if they weren't quality tatters! Draggins of silks and satins, oh fine stuff. Much too fine for a poor negro slave-girl to be wearin on her back. And that's a fact. Tho' I admired her jackdaw cunning in makin off with'em, and so I did!

And so he did, George Augustus 'Hercules' Adams. The Lord bless him for his base-born ignorance, his servile heart, and low-down native cunning, the rogue! For it can in truth be said that experience is a great thing, if not too dearly bought.

Come, let me tilt the mirror to fall more kindly upon this sylvan scene: Look, there he stands, naked at the top half, but for an old straw hat upon his head. Light falls through the brim of the hat, the holey brim and casts a net-like shadow over half his face. The cold pink of his mouth moves, and I think of the fish. Poor fish! And of the man as fish; and of myself as a fisher of men. A blasphemous thought but one which, (in view of my own sad history) affords me solace, and I laugh out loud: ha, ha, ha, drowning the fellow's words, and causing his mouth to fall open in surprise. Though showman that he is, he recovers quickly enough and joins in my merriment. That's it, he cries. That's the way of it. Oh yes, my bright eyed beauty, yes!

Then he grasped at my shoulders with his hands, his blood warm hands that were safe as death; and tried to make me dance the dance. The old dance of Eve and Adam in that woodland spot. I saw the leaves, blackly patterned against the blue sky looking upwards. The sky was a deep, a perfect blue, and the leaves showed blackly against it, like holes in a fabric torn — then the red light dancing — Lord!

For the briefest of moments, I struggled against a feeling of helplessness — such complete and utter helplessness as threatened to overwhelm me entirely. But, the gods being with me in force, I all of a sudden took heart, and gathering my wits and strength about me (for he was a puny enough fellow all told) I wrenched myself violently free of him — hissing, in as deadly a voice as I could muster: *Quam vis ille niger quam vis tu Candidus essus*, oaf!

It was enough.

And in the terrible stillness that followed, it came on to rain. A golden shower of rain it seemed, with the small rain steadily falling, while the sun shone mildly through. Oh, blessed rain, the bright drops fell on my upturned face and covered it, like so many coins.

Well, well, they say that gold doth blindeth the eye...

Indeed, and in his case, stupefy the heart? That conning man! My guinea gold, he called me then, his little treasure, and many

44

other wearisome endearments besides; until at last, perceiving my continued coldness, he left off as suddenly as he'd began; and, moving away from me, commenced to busy himself with a variety of traps and boxes.

Jest leave her be an' she'll come round, says I to myself. They allus do, or they don't. Can't be holding with — Yet who'd have thought it, eh? A learned negro-girl, fallen into your path, a scholard, no less, that's what you've stumbled on. A phee-nom-enon! Stap me if she ain't with all them words. All them latin words that came a-tumbling from her mouth! I shakes my head an' smiles at the wonderful workin's of providence. And in my mind's eye, straight ahead I can see the letterin' (red 'n' gold ornamented) bold spread across: PRODIGY OF NATURE! (most recently discovered, lost and found a-wandering, in old England's woods) Proprietor: Geo. A. Adams, esq.

I shakes my head and smiles again, because that ain't the half of it. Oh no. So missish in her ways, M'lady, so refined an' delicate seeming withal, an' yet — this being the great beauty, the contrariness of the situation — her's nothing but a black gal! Which puts a werry different sort of complexion on things as you might say...

With that I leaves off rootling in my boxes and turns upon her, grinning. What d'ye think of this then, Miss? says I hoisting one of my catches above my head.

Stand off from me with that vile serpent, she cries. (For it's a snake, an adder that I'm waving aloft.) Keep your distance, simpleton — hold!

Such commandment in her voice she has, the black girl. Such clear, bell-like tones! It's more 'n enough to make a humble showman like myself fall back in his tracks, an I does. But only so far. For I'm a wonderful courageous man, I am. Oh, yes! I can take any amount of female belabourin', almost without flinchin'.

Now don't you be afeared young Miss, says I, in a calmish tone of voice. See here, I've taken the stingers out — 'tis quite safe. And I smiles at the girl werry nice, at the same time as I squeedges its tail, the snake's. I mean really pincers it a'tween my thumb and forefinger so as to make it twist and curl its body round my upper half. Then I strikes up a pose, like so.

I'm makin' like a statue, can't you see? he cried. A living breathin' statue. Putting on the old heroic.

The snake, a deep, blackish green in colouring, slid across the fellow's neck and shoulders as he stood there grinning. He held up one arm. The arm was deathly white, and the snake entwined itself around it, like a beautifully jewelled arm-bracelet of jade and ebony. A look of simple pride came over the man's face as he witnessed my complete, albeit unwilling, fascination. Please to see! Please to see! he cried in his showman's voice. And for my next trick! Whereupon he again took the snake by the tip of its tail and, opening wide his mouth, allowed the creature to inch its way down the column of his throat, until it all but disappeared.

Well, talk about blench! You'd have sworn black was the white of the negro-girl's eye when she see'd me do that. No sooner the snake goes down past my swallow, (which is the ticklish bit) then she starts to retchin'. I could hear her heavin' her very guts up almost, to judge by the noises she was makin'. And when at last I draws un out, neat and nasty as it is, I has to smile — to see her sat, with her two hands clapped across her mouth and her black eyes starin'.

Why bless you! I whispers in a hoarse voice. It don't do no harm, no it don't. Not a bit of it. Tho' the taste's a bit queer, a bit roughish on the tongue, I adds for honesty's sake. Yet if I was to scrape off the slime with my fingernail — see how it comes away, look? Why then I'd swear at 'Nize yon snake's the cleanest creature that ever was put on this earth. So 'elp me God!

So saying, he curled the snake tenderly and laid it away in its box. That done, he looked about him for the fish and stashed that away also. Taking care, I noticed, to cover its fat, silvery gleam with an abundance of moss and leaves. During this time he spoke not a word, but occasionally adopting a mournful expression on his face, he pursed his lips and gave out a high, plaintive whistle. And eerie it was indeed to hear, floating out from the dark surrounding woods, the feathered response in kind. As for myself, he seemed to have forgotten my existence entirely — until at last, having fastened up the buttons on his coarse brown jacket, he turned to me and smiled: Shall you come along with me then, shall you?

I have the sound of his voice by me now. Echoing through time, that wheedling voice, with its reverberating call of: *shall you? shall you? shall you?*

And my response?

So many thoughts and images — a tumult of thoughts and voices and images, all crowding in on me now as I bring back the moment.

Not two feet from me, the man stands, waiting. His watery eyes are small and ill-set in his head, no fishpools of Heshbon they, yet small though they are, they shine bright with confidence. He tips me the wink and smiles. You come along with me, he says, and we shall turn a pretty penny, you and I — drawing in the crowds at fair-time.

Why, at the Womberwell's Menagerie of Beasts and Birds, we should be a champion turn, you and I. Champion!

I listened as he continued talking, a stream of words – such grand, foolish words! Such a rosy picture as was painted for me, that I in my drifting state, was only too eager to believe in, to collude with — for I had risen from the weeds undrowned, and now found myself in changed mood — standing on the cusp of a new way of life, a new beginning...

In short, I assented to his proposals and threw in my lot with him, this snake-man, bird-man, adam-man and thief. And as we set off towards the great city of London and its environs, I remember glancing upwards and catching, just, the ragged winged soaring of a bird into the blue beyond. There were red streaks of cloud on either side as I looked upwards, and these clouds seemed to part the sky — east and west, like the great red swags of a curtain.

What course of events, what ill wind had driven me thus far, my reader will perhaps be asking? What hurts, what injustices had been suffered by me, sufficient to explain my taking that most precipitous of steps — that is, of leaving the protection of my Great-Uncle's house, and turning myself voluntarily out of doors, there to flounder in the wide world, and I a female, black and penniless? Ah therein lies the tale! But shall I make a hedge of my thorns, or a crown? My objective in setting down this history, has been in the way of an attempt to possess, rather than be possessed by it.

Extract from a diary (as nearly as can be remembered):

> Caenwood, August 29th 1779
>
> A black came in after dinner and sat with the ladies and after coffee walked with the company in the gardens... She is neither handsome nor genteel — pert enough. I knew her history before, but My Lord mentioned it again. His nephew, Sir John Lindsay, having taken her mother prisoner in a Spanish vessel, brought her to England where she was delivered of this girl, of which she was then with child, and which was taken care of by Lord Mansfield, and has been educated by his family. He calls her Dido, which I suppose is all the name she has.

Liar! I remember thinking as I read the above (and I should not have read it, but that is another story), liar! Liar! For I knew well enough the facts of my own history and that what had been set down by this diarist was but a wicked fabrication, a tissue of lies and half truths! My mother was indeed a poor black slave, *'stolen from Afric's fancied happy seat'*. But as to my father — why my father was none other than the Englishman who had taken her captive: that same Sir John Lindsay who was Knight of the Bath, Rear Admiral of the Red — and nephew of Lord Mansfield, the Lord Chief Justice of England, the highest judge in the land. *I knew her history but my lord mentioned it again!* It took some time for me to realise that the source, the disseminator of those falsehoods concerning my history and birth, was none other than my own Great-Uncle! A crushing blow also to realise the painful, the inescapable fact that in so doing he had denied me, his own flesh and blood! My unhappiness on reaching these conclusions was very great — almost insupportable...

Heigh-ho! I see you hiding there behind the screen, says Master Smith, come a-poking his head round. Why, says he, snatching up some of my papers: Dido? Elizabeth? Belle? What a lot of names you have given yourself!

That's right, Sir, says I, taking care to grab the papers back, and hold them safely. Black Bet's been called a few things in her time, and so she has.

Oh I should not call you *Black Bet*, says the boy very seriously (for he is a nice boy, very grave and studious in his ways), I should rather call you 'Bronze' given that your colouring has that tincture of olive in it — I b'lieve that is the classical appellation — 'Bronze'.

Why bless you Master Smith, then Bronze it is.And you shall not mind it?

Mind it? Why not at all Sir, says I with a smile. Nay, not at all, for I am what I am – which is to say that I'm one of life's chancelings, as you might call it — a bastard — begging your parsnips, that's what I am. An' I'm smart as a carrot, newly scraped!

GONE FOR A SONG

Bomb! bomb! bomb!
> *bomb-bee-doo-wah!*
Yea! yea! yea!
> *yea, yea.*
Woe! woe! woe!
> *woe-bee-doo-wah*
aaah

Only the lonely. I likes that song, I likes it. Mister Robert Banks next door is singing that song. To his self, without any words, just the tune you can hear. Buzzing out from under his breath as he walks along. Like a fly or a bee buzzing, I thinks, as I watches him walk. Up and down their back-garden path, he dips his hand into a duffle-bag and throws, as far as the wire-netting on our side. It's white lime it is, he's throwing. And it stays on top of the brown soil where he's dug it over, like icing sugar on a wedding cake, white. Nothing ever grows in Mister Banks' garden, apart from the weeds and stingy nettles, and grass that blows like long strands of hair, uprooted now on the concrete, with the clumps of earth around them.

Mister Banks must have started digging the garden really early this morning. He was there when Mama drew back the curtains. 'Christ, he's up early,' Mama said. 'He must want something to do.'

The wind makes me shiver. I looks up at the sky and sees it stretched out, pale blue and shiny cold, like the satin on my bedspread. Mama got me that bedspread from the catalogue, to go with my new fold-up bed when we moved here. Out here, people say, or out there. How long you been living out there then, with all that fresh air? D'you like it?

It's far away from Town, where we lived before. I can see fields from where I'm standing. At the bottom end of all the back-gardens, rising up. And there's a river down there somewhere, that I can't see, and that I'm not allowed to go by. But I can see the fields, they go up over the hills like the squares on a blanket. There are cows inside one of the fields, lying down. The big black patches on their backs look like 2,4, 6, 8, 10,12,14 — fifteen Africas painted in ink on their creamy white backs, like maps. I've never seen a cow, up close. They look to be as big as dogs from here.

As big as Sheba, say, who is Joey Banks' alsatian; and who is nosing her way along the garden path, sniffing and scratching at the lime. 'Shebuh!' Mister Banks shouts, turning round. 'She-buh!' Sheba takes her leathery nose away from the lime, and backs off into her corner by the wall. Sheba's coat is smooth and dark, but the fur down her jaws and her front is a scrubby yellow, like the fur on the inside of a sheepskin jacket. And her eyes are green, mineral green, my mother says. Sometimes, Sheba frightens me with those eyes, sometimes she looks at you empty with those eyes, as if they've never seen a person before. That's because Sheba's not human, she's an animal who's been tamed, and her eyes are mineral.

'I'll give you, girl. I'll give you' — Mister Banks stands over Sheba until she flattens her ears and squeezes her eyes shut. Then he turns back to his throwing, like the lemon haired man in my bible picture book: The Sower of Seed. Mr Banks looks dead alike him to me, even though he wears eye-glasses, and squirts hair-oil on his yellow hair to comb it into a teddy boy quiff. 'Trying to keep up with Marty,' Mama says. 'That's all.'

'*Maybee toomorow*' — Mister Banks is singing higher now, high and sad, like a question mark to the sky: '*wunnoo ro-mance?*'

Marty is Mister Banks' wife, but she doesn't live with him and Joey any more. Not since she walked out and left them, more

51

than a week ago. Mama said she heard voices, and banging and screaming in the night. I tried to remember if I'd heard anything, but there was nothing there when I tried to remember, only silence.

Mister Banks has stopped singing now and everything's gone quiet. A Sunday quiet. That's because Joey's still at Mass, serving on the altar as an altar boy. Huh! I picture them standing around the tabernacle which is sparkling white and shaped like a bee-hive. The tabernacle has a little green door in the middle, ready for all the sins of the world to fly inside as soon as the priest unlatches it: 'Thou who takest away the sins of the world,' the congregation will shout out, 'have mercy on us!'

I drops my head. There's a mortal sin on my soul. Another one for missing Mass, because Mama says she can't be dragging two small kids and a heavy push-chair all the way to Church on a Sunday, it's too much. I drops my head even further, and sees the ants crawling over the concrete cement, like sins.

Mister Banks has finished with the lime. He's stepping back now, to see. The duffle-bag's swinging empty from his hands, and the garden is completely white. A small brown bird flies down from the wire-netting, and hops near the edge of the lime. When it turns round, I can't believe my eyes. A robin red breast! with a splash of orange red down its head and front, like tomato soup from a tin. As if the bird has dipped its head and chest in a tin of tomato soup.

I take a leaf from one of our geraniums, and crush it into tiny pieces in my hand. Mister Banks' garden is as beautiful as a Christmas card, with the lime sparkling white as snow, and the robin red breast perched upon it. But that picture's only there for a moment. Then zonk! the bird falls over. Like a toy bird, zonk. Joey Banks has gone and fired a shot from his bow and arrow, straight at the bird. I didn't hear the window open, or see him take aim. I only saw the arrow, whizzing down, zonk! The robin is lying with its red breast face up to the sky, but its wings are fluttering, it must still be alive.

52

'Did I gerrit dad? Did I gerrit?'

Joey Banks is leaning out of his bedroom window, trying to see. And there's a tinny taste in my mouth, like the taste of blood, but from the geraniums.

'Orr!' he shouts. 'Orr, what! Bulls-eye!'

'You mind you don't fall,' says Mister Banks, turning round and shouting up at him. 'Otherwise you'll know it.' Then he turns back to the garden and the bird. But the robin has dragged its body off the ground and it's flying crazy now, zooming this way and that. Mister Banks ducks twice, but Sheba sits up straight and snaps at the bird, as if it's no more than a fly. Then all of a sudden the bird just stops. Its wings are whirring but its body just stops and drops like a stone.

There's a very small crunch. Mr Banks has stepped on its head, I think he must have. I can hear him scraping his boot along the concrete. Cleaning it off. I look across. He looks up and sees me looking, Mister Banks. Then he makes a face at me and smiles, as if he's swallowed something horrible but good for him, like syrup of figs. 'You didn't see none of that, did you, my love?' I shake my head slowly back and fore, as if I didn't.

'Good. That's not for little girls to see, that's not.' Mister Banks walks over to the wire-netting and stands there, smiling down at me. His eyes behind his eye-glasses are far back in his head, like silvery nails shining. And I wonders why his hands don't hurt, pressing into the wire-netting like that. They should be bleeding. 'Are you all right, my love?' he says. 'Are you all right?'

Then the next thing I know is, Mister Banks is over our back-garden fence large as life, thumping on the back-door for Mama to let me in. He has to bang a few times, waiting. Then Mama's standing there on the top step, looking down at him, and he's stood talking up at her, and smiling over my head at her, to show it's nothing serious, though his voice is low and serious. 'She's a bit upset she is,' he says. 'There's been a little—' and he tells about the bird. Then Mama says to me: 'Oh come on inside then, you silly you!' And their voices go on talking as I walk past. I hear them saying: 'It's all right, yes.' Then, 'No, I know. Sensitive, awful sensitive. Takes everything to heart. It's true they do. These days.' And Mister Banks laughs small and says aye. 'Oh aye, and not like my little blighter. I don't know who he — him, not me. No, nothing.' And laughs, 'Ah, well.'

Then they go on talking about something different, so I push open the door to the living room and walk inside. It's warm, inside, lovely and warm. There's a nice fire in the grate and Baby-boy is asleep in his cot. When I try to straighten out his fat little legs he starts to grizzle. So I shove the big blue dummy in his mouth quick and he nods off again. Lucky for me. 'You tormenting little mare you,' Mama would have said. 'Disturbing him when he was asleep!' Baby-boy is the apple of Mama's eye, she says so.

I lift the net curtain by the window, but there's nothing hardly to see. The arrow is still there, the rubber sucker on the pointed end makes a small spot of red against the white; but I can't see the bird. I wonder where its body's gone? And Mama's still out there talking — it's ages before I hear her shut the back-kitchen door and come inside. When I hear the door slam shut, I step in front of the net curtains quick, pretending not to know she's there. '*Call for the robin redbreast and the wren,*' I says in a small sad voice, like they taught us in school. '*Since o'er shady groves they hover, and with leaves and flowers do cover —*' Then I stop and huff on the glass, to see my face go all white and ghostly.

'Come away from that window,' Mama says. 'And sit down by the fire; showing off! I thought you was supposed to be sick?' But I stay where I am, and soon she's standing behind me.

'Ma, Mama?'

I'm standing there looking up at her, waiting for her to look down at me, but she won't. Not yet. She's tall, my mother is, her nose can reach the white metal cross part of the window frame, even when she's wearing mules, like she is now. Her hair is soft and brown, with kinks in it. And although she always tells me

54

she's not made of money, right now she looks as though she is, with the sunshine streaming cold and yellow on her face, then setting hard, like money. A foreign coin I thinks, similar to the one my dad left in his pocket when he flew to Canada. My dad had an accident in Canada. They sent us a letter in a 'registered envelope' telling us he wouldn't be home for 'some time'. Mama cried when she read the letter. Baby-boy cried too. He has the ˜ame kind of face as hers. Glinty-gold, while mine is as brown as a penny, like my dad's.

'Ma.' I pull on her cardigan. 'Joey Banks woan go to heaven will he, aiming at birds? Mister Banks won't either, Ma? I saw him, stepping on its head eugh! He's a murderer.'

'Now that's enough, now,' Mama says and drops the curtain. 'Come on and help me tidy the front room,' she says. 'Come on quick before the baby wakes up.'

I like to help Mama with the tidying. I sort all the little things my dad's sent from abroad, while she moves the heavy furniture round. Around and around, til everything's standing in a different place to what it was the Sunday before. I give a little skip and start to follow her across the room, but something makes me stop and turn back to the window. A funny thought comes into my head and out of my mouth before I can stop it. 'Marty's over there in the garden,' I say pointing. 'Look.' Mama clumps back on her mules to see. Then she gives a small laugh, 'Oh, you lying little Mary, you,' she says. 'There's no one out there — you're having me on!' And it's true, there's no-one out there. Only the empty sky, and the lime white garden, with the grass sticking out of the clumps of earth in the corner, like strands of hair.

I'm wicked I am, telling lies. Lies turn into sins and cloud up your soul. I told a lie at home and in school: 'Hands up all those who went to Mass on Sunday?' 'Miss!' my hand goes up. And no-one knows, that I never. But God knows, and it's on my conscience. And in assembly, in the middle of prayers — in the middle of: *'to thee do we cry, poor banished children of Eve, to thee do we send up our sighs'* — something made me stop. And I

55

opened my eyes and saw the bees. A swarm of bees swarming outside the hall windows. There was a humming in my ears which was 'Hail Holy Queen'. But the bees were silent. They didn't look like bees they looked like flakes of snow speckling the sky behind the glass. And dancing up and down as they came nearer, the way snowflakes do, all the time they're falling.

When it was going home time, I ran all the way, because I wanted to tell Mama about the bees. But when I opened the front room door, I saw Mr Banks kneeling in front of our radiogramme, with a screw-driver in his hands. I jumped back when I opened the door and saw him kneeling there on our carpet with a screw-driver in his hands. 'Oh Joey?' he was saying. 'He's gone to stay with his grandmother, he have. Just for the time being —' Then he smiled over his shoulder at me: 'Yer comes trouble! Let's make way for trouble,' he said, and laughed.

I thought he'd go home once he fixed the pick-up on the radiogramme, but he didn't. After tea, he sat in my dad's chair with a glass and a bottle of Mackeson in his hands waiting for the records to fall, one by one. There were seven records all together, and every time a record dropped, Mr Banks poured more drink into his glass and sipped. Sometimes I watched the records turning round and around; and sometimes I looked at the glass in Mr Banks' hands. His fingers were like white stubs behind the brown of the glass, pressing.

Then the last record dropped, and I sat up straight and listened. But I fell asleep with my eyes half open, Mama said, listening to a song about the moon and the river — *Moonriver* that played on and on and on. Until the moon turned into a record label, white and round. And the river was the record, shining black and winding round and round and round —

Until I woke up in my pull-out bed, and it was funny because everything was still instead of turning. And I thought about the moon and the river here on earth, turning. Then Sheba started barking, and I looked out through the window. I saw the moon. It was round and wispy white, with bald grey patches on it, like a tennis ball someone had thrown. That's why she was barking, the dog; and jumping up and down. She didn't know like I did, that it was really the moon, and not a tennis ball that someone had thrown.

Then the back-door to Mister Banks' house flew open all of a sudden and I heard him shouting for her to get inside. Then I laid back down and went to sleep.

And in the morning it was Sunday and we went to Mass, me, Mama and Baby-boy, all together and I was happy, and my dad came home — no. The time... is like a record turning I thinks, slowly at first then faster and faster once you know the tune. Though the time it takes to turn is always the same, really.

It was Marty who came home first. We didn't even know she was back, until we saw her and Mister Banks, standing in their garden amongst the weeds, having their picture taken by Joey. The three of them were wearing plaid shirts and blue jeans with the cuffs turned up, and Marty had her hair in a pony-tail.

'Look at them,' Mama said, when she saw them out there. 'They looks like something out of *Okla*-bloody-*holma* doan they? Dressed like that.' Then my dad came home from Canada with his leg in plaster, and we were a happy family too.

He brought us toys and Baby-boy crawled on the carpet and played with his toy husky, while my dad laid down on the settee to rest his leg; and I brushed his hair for him. 'I bet you missed me,' he said to Mama, while I brushed his hair for him. 'Serafina, did your mother miss me?' he said smiling across the room at her. 'I bet she did.'

'She cried,' I said. 'Soon as she opened the registered envelope. Boo-hoo, hoo.' I pretended to rub my eyes with my fists, and peeped to see if my dad was laughing, 'Boo-hoo, hoo!' My dad laid his head back on the settee, and smiled up at the ceiling. Then he closed his eyes. I wanted to make him smile some more, so I told him about Mister Banks coming in to fix the radiogramme and everything.

When I came upstairs the baby was crying, and I could hear

banging and screaming and something went smash. 'It's all coming out now, oh yes. Break these things and you'll pay for 'em. Money? It's my money, keeping you and these kids. Well who brought them up then? Not you! If it'd been anybody else, anybody else but that whey-faced sonofabitch.'

'What — what? You're crazy you are. Crazy taking notice of a little kid.'

The sky was grey and empty when I came upstairs, but it's snowing now, I think. The snowflakes fill the sky like a swarm of bees, looking to settle. When they do, our garden will be covered, completely.

DIGGING FOR VICTORY

When Mr Churchill's war-ship sailed into Cardiff Docks in the spring of 1955, I was seventeen years old and working at my first job, as a clerk in the Ministry of Labour, right on the corner of Custom House Street and Canal Parade.

Of course I loved it there, though that time of year can be very blowy, with the March winds coming off the sea and roaring around us. Like a great sea-lion, I used to think, grey and submerged, then rearing up to poke cold blue eyes in the sky. In the evenings the winds would die down and the sky was often chemically pink. Then warm sea breezes would bring the smell of fish from around the comer in Mill Lane, and I'd walk home, happy to have done a good day's work for a good day's pay.

I was proud to have a job up town. Stepping over Canal Parade Bridge into town made me different. Teeny said it made me stuck up. 'Miss High and Mighty' she'd say, looking down at the brass buttons on my navy coat. 'Miss Piss-pot, who you thinks you are I'm sure I doan know.'

Teeny was only fifteen and she worked with all the other coloured girls down Oram's, making lavatory brushes in the winter and artificial Christmas trees in the summer. I mean, she *did* work there, for a time, clamping the wire twists and dipping the bristles into the vats of green dye, to make them into Christmas trees. She left after less than a year though, claiming that the tips of her fingers were turning indelible green.

I felt I had to say something that Friday night, after she'd waltzed into the room and thrown her wage packet on the table. 'Teeny,' I said quietly, 'are you quite sure you want to work?'

'Of course I wanna work,' she said, taking a bottle of nail

varnish from her handbag and bracing her feet against the arm of the settee. 'I just doan fancy getting poisoned, that's all.'

'Teeny,' my voice was patient, 'green doesn't necessarily mean gangrene, poisoning that is. Have you tried using half a lemon?'

But she was busy painting her toe-nails scarlet and didn't even bother to raise her head. In the event, she was only out of work for a fortnight, not long enough to claim U.A.B., thank goodness, when Mrs Cheng offered her a job in the steam-room of the Chinese laundry. So she went down there to 'slave' as she put it, almost on the dockside, next to the sea.

I think about Teeny as I stand in the kitchen, ironing my white blouse ready for work, and listening to Mr Churchill's voice on the wireless. He is talking about 'this island race' and the 'dawning of the second age of Elizabeth'. Mr Churchill says we are the new Elizabethans, we English-speaking peoples, bound by the crimson thread of kinship. 'The crimson thread of kinship' stays in my mind. I think about its meaning as Teeny flounces into the kitchen, way late for work and wrapped in mother's paradise blue kimono. A present sent by father from sea.

'Aren't you going in then?' I ask, careful not to look up, concentrating on smoothing the creases from the sleeve of my blouse. 'Mrs Cheng will dock you an hour, won't she, if you're more than ten minutes late?' Instead of answering, she marches straight to the dresser and starts to fiddle with the dial on the wireless. Mr Churchill's voice is drowned in a crackle of static. 'Teeny!' I say sharply, 'I was listening to that! It's the Prime Minister, talking to us.'

'Us!' she says, flapping the silken arms of her kimono and mooching around the table with her eyes closed. Music from the American Forces Network fills the air.

'Turn that down, please.'

'What?' She looks at me with pitying eyes. Enviously I see how the darkness of her skin kills the gaudy blue of the kimono. Of the two of us, Teeny is the one who most resembles father.

I walk to work on my own. Half-way across the bridge I slow

down and look over the side. The water in the canal is opaque, it is impossible to see in. My eyes trail the line of chickweed and dead grass up the canal bank and into the first of the bombed out houses. A small tree has forced its way up through the floorboards of a wall-papered room. Someone has propped a newspaper placard beneath its flourishing umbrella of dark green leaves: 'Cardiff prepares for G.O.M.'. G.O.M? I'm half-way down the road before it clicks, Grand Old Man. 'Cardiff prepares for Grand Old Man!'

Inside the office, there is an air of quiet excitement. Edna holds up the front page of her morning paper when we stop for elevenses. 'Look at him, Kay, doesn't he look wonderful?'

'He looks marvellous,' says Kay, peering over Edna's shoulder. 'Have you seen this, Mr Norman?'

Both Kay and Edna are ex-Land Army, while Mr Norman saw service in North Africa. Now he ambles over and stands between them moving his lips as he reads down the column inches.

'Interesting, that,' he says, taking out his pipe. 'Interesting. I know for a fact that Mr Churchill's nanny was a lady named Everest, Nurse Everest. And look at this now,' Mr Norman taps the page with the stem of his pipe, 'it says here that the great man is being looked after in his *entourage*, by a nurse called McAlpine. Only a little thing but —'

Everyone exclaims at the coincidence, then Mr Norman looks up at the skylight. 'Oh-oh, ladies! Here comes some of your favourite liquid again.' He means that it's starting to rain. There is a pause as we listen to the rain falling on the skylight. Then Edna blows her nose. 'Our climate is changing,' she says slowly, 'there can be no doubt about that.' I meet her glance with a cheery smile. 'Ah well,' she scrapes back her chair. 'This won't buy baby a new pair of shoes, will it? Now then Kay, what are you having with your tea, buttered bun?'

The war-ship pulled into Cardiff dock just before mid-day. At tea-time, sitting in the kitchen at home, Teeny said the girls in work had stacked bales of laundry in front of the high windows, then they'd taken it in turns to climb up and look out. I asked if they'd seen the Prime Minister? No. First, they saw the flowers, she said. Trail after trail of hot house pinks and giant orchids. Then there were the animals, some feathered, and some furred — and silver buckets of ice. Oh, and live red lobsters, ready for the pot. All trundled up the gang plank by Malayan sailors in dazzling white sailor-suits.

'Have you left anything out?' asked mother kindly; and Teeny laughed. She said the Prime Minister had to have his food killed fresh, it was doctor's orders. 'You didn't see Mr Churchill at all then?' I was highly suspicious. Teeny said she'd caught a glimpse. They brought him up on deck for a short while. A fattish figure, lying in a basket-chair with a black silk cloth over his face.

'That was how he used to take a nap during the war,' said mother, 'with a black silk cloth over his face.'

Teeny said she'd thought he was deado, until the cloth fell off and she saw his eyes, looking up at her. But a nurse had bent down and covered his face again.

That evening after supper, the three of us took a walk as far as the esplanade wall, and stood with crowds of other people, watching. There was no sign of the Prime Minister, but the ship beamed its searchlights over the black waters of the estuary, and we could hear music coming from the port-holes on the far side. Mother held a hand up to her ear and nudged us both. '*Eldorado Man*,' she whispered, 'by Harry James and his orchestra.' At nine o'clock it began to rain; and the people standing in front of us opened their umbrellas very slowly, as if they were in a dream. As we turned to go, we caught the scent of something rotting on the wind and wondered what it was.

Coming down for work next morning, I was surprised to see mother turn from the front doorstep with an anxious look on her face. A large car was moving down our street, slow as a hearse, and a voice was blaring out. I recognised the voice immediately. 'What's he doing here?' I cried, running to the door and looking out. Mother told me to hush, and I realised the car was empty, apart from the chauffeur. Mr Churchill's voice was coming from a kind of loud-hailer, shaped like an enormous gramophone-horn and attached to the roof of the car. Up and down our street, people were standing on their doorsteps, listening anxiously.

The Prime Minister's voice was tremulous, but unmistakable. His recorded message was brief. The war-ship had collided with the inner gates of the old sea-lock during the night. The gates had collapsed and the canal waters had emptied into the sea. He was calling on all able-bodied persons to offer their services in what was shaping up to be a great task of reclamation. 'A task which might prove to be of immense importance in the trying times ahead... This is a test of our national character... Our resolve... You should come prepared to toil, sweat...' His voice continued to echo in the streets around us, right up as far as the green domed mosque in Sophia Street, where the words came out in Arabic. Then there was silence.

We came in and closed the door, wondering what to do for the best. Mother said she couldn't afford to give up her office cleaning, she was late enough as it was. I was unsure as to how best to proceed though I recognised the nature of what was being asked. 'Go in to work first,' said mother, 'that way you'll get paid whatever happens.'

Teeny was sitting on a stool in the back kitchen, straightening her hair with the hot-iron straightening comb. She looked up when I told her what had happened. Then she opened her mouth wide like a cat, and yawned. She asked if I had any hair grips she could borrow so she could pin back the sides and roll what was left into a bang.

I remember the trouble I had trying to get into work, that morning. Crowds of people swept past me as I reached Canal Parade Bridge. Most of them carried gardening implements: rakes and shovels, picks and hoes. They all strode past, like a shabby, but purposeful, army. Then I saw Mr Norman standing under the railway arch with Kay and Edna. The three of them were wearing military looking duffle coats, the colour of wet sand, with red plaid lining in the hoods. Mr Norman was carrying a pair of binoculars, which he raised to his eyes every now and then, carefully surveying the crowds. Before the binoculars reached me, I turned, as if in a dream, and joined the flow.

By mid-morning, a system of sorts had been set up, and by the early afternoon the task of reclamation was well under way. The canal looked like a huge valley, its sloping sides crowded with wellingtoned figures sifting through the soft greenish black mud. The water had gone, emptied violently into the sea, and the violence of its going had transformed the area into an enormous excavation site, leaving a mangle of objects half exposed to the light. I remember water wheels and iron wheels and cast iron plate. And heavy, rusted chains endlessly uncurling out of the mud, like snakes being stirred from hibernation. Other things, more minuscule in size, grew into oxidised hills as nails and rivets, nuts and bolts, were salvaged by the bucketful and heaped. It was an exhumation of the industrial past. Layer by layer.

As a government employee, it was my duty to identify and record all findings. It was tedious and dirty unpleasant work, but it had to be done. Everything had to be listed, then taken away for deposition in the huge bins marked 'reclamation'. The biggest find came towards the end of the afternoon, when a group of business wallahs dug up an enormous set of gear-wheels. They had their picture taken standing by the wheels, smiling proudly, their shirt sleeves rolled up, oblivious of the smells that permeated the air as the sun came out and shone on the black, putrescent muck.

As for me, I experienced a moment of happiness and contentment as I looked about me. Giant loading cranes jutted out against the sky-line like the vertebrae of prehistoric animals. The seagulls dipped and swooped; and the trucks made mournful shunting noises as they rolled up and down the sidings. Here and there I saw coloured people, Docks people like myself, helping with the task in hand. It was just like the war-time, I thought, when Britain would have stood alone, if the Empire hadn't rushed to her aid. Jamaica was the first with the spitfire fund! Our family

64

would always remember that, and father had gloried in it. From one small island to the mother island, it was a gesture that would never be forgotten, father said so.

The operation was wound down gradually. At five o'clock a hooter was sounded and someone threw a stretch of green tarpaulin across the mud. A car drew up and an official from the Department of Public Works got out and made a speech. It was the Dunkirk spirit all over again, he said, and wonderful to see. Wonderful! He raised his arms as if to embrace us. 'People of Cardiff, go home now; and take a well earned rest. Thank you and God bless.'

I walked over to where Kay and Edna were standing with Mr Norman. Edna was holding something small and heavy in her arms. 'Just look what I've found,' she hissed, 'an iron lion! Try saying that when you've had a few.' She glanced towards the official, who was getting into his car and said she'd heard a rumour that Mr Churchill might yet be arriving in person. Edna looked towards the horizon as she spoke, but it remained empty.

'Oh what I wouldn't give to see him,' she said. 'Or even fox-faced Mr Attlee for that matter.'

'Or handsome Mr Eden,' said Kay, wistfully.

Mr Norman lit his pipe. 'Ours is not to reason why.'

'Yes, I know,' said Edna softly, 'ours is but to — isn't it, Monty?' She nestled her face against the little lion in her arms.

'Very appropriate name,' said Mr Norman, 'very appropriate.'

Teeny was unimpressed when I recounted my story to mother, late that night. 'The more fool you,' she chipped in. 'Fancy handing over all the scrap iron. I'd have kept it. You were entitled. It was treasure trove.'

'But that's why Mr Churchill made his special appeal, Teeny,' I said. 'On behalf of the nation. All that stuff was needed. Urgently.'

'Needed for what?' she asked nastily. 'An iron curtain?'

Even mother had to smile at this, though she told Teeny that that was enough. She could see I was a bit tired and crestfallen.

A few days later, there were pictures of Mr Churchill on all the front pages, standing at the doorway of Number Ten, waving to the crowds. The hand with the famous cigar was held aloft, and he was wearing pyjamas and a white towelled bathrobe. I thought his eyes looked strangely vacant and subdued. The newspapers said that a common cold had occasioned the Prime Minister's recent absence from the public eye. That was all. Yet by the beginning of April they were announcing his resignation.

The Department of Public Works had the canal filled in and eventually renamed 'Churchill Way' in his honour. As a busy thorough-fare, it has two distinguishing features: a very long traffic island, and a single stunted palm-tree dotting its centre.

T.I.N.A.

At the end of my first day Philip said: How did it go? And straight off, I put my hand up to my forehead and said, *Don't*— because you don't, do you? Want to talk about it. Not for those first few days?

But that was — oh I don't know how long ago that was — yet here we are already look, with a day off. A day off! One of those amazing, natural occurrences that happen to anyone in gainful employment. That was the thought that struck me, when I opened my eyes this morning. The sheer beauty of it struck me and I said: Dorothy, you're gunna have to pinch yourself old girl, because you're back, in the swim of things. Having this day off proves it. Amazing really, to find yourself back in the working world, when you thought you'd had your chips... didn't you?

I'm fifty-nine years old. Now, I know what you're thinking, but it's not like that. I've always worked, right throughout our married life. (We haven't any kids; the doctor advised not — cobalt treatment — Philip's.) It's just that I never thought of myself as *being* fifty-nine until we decided to move back here, and I found myself standing on top of a metal grating outside the Job Centre, looking at all those little cards they slot in the windows. You know the ones?

Loads of them. I must've stood there for ever such a long time, reading through. And I kept thinking, that's no good, and that's no good. Suitable for under twenty-five, under forty? Now that was a bit more hopeful —? I leaned forward a step, but there was a face. My own, mooned in the glass in front of me, 'n I thought my god, Dodo, you're gunna have to tell some real porkers, aren't you girl? I mean there was no escaping it. My face was there in the glass in front of me. Those big-boned features bland enough, yes. But creaking with age, especially round the eyes. I've got these rather small eyes because of the big face, I always thought. Hurrp! Their colour? A very nice topaz, but tiny like sultanas. Peeping between those cards that said wanted! wanted! wanted! And I was hopping like mad from foot to foot, saying, that's all very well, and that's as may be, but are they gunna want me, eh? Hurrp!

In the end, a rather nice looking chap, whom I hadn't realised was there, turned round and said, Look, just say "yes" to whatever question they ask you! Rather a nice looking chap too... and that gave me a boost — well it does, doesn't it? So I thought come on girl, roll up your sleeves and get in there! But you mustn't encourage me, I know how I tend to go on... on and on.

Look at the time. And what have I done with my day off so far? Well, Philip went out to work early, then Piddles came in bed and snuggled up to me. He waits till he goes out, you see. Then, let me think, I had two lots of tea and toast, mmmn. Then I stayed in bed until half nine — gone half nine it was — re-reading *Little Lord Fauntleroy*, bliss. But I must get out now, and do a bit of shopping, not that there are many shops up here. There's only the one big store. Tesco's. Semolina, 2lbs for 48p, that's not bad is it? Saw it as the bus went past yesterday, and made a note.

Ours is a one bedroomed house, all the houses on our side are either one or two bedrooms. *Eden-grove, Chez-nous, Ferny-hough Valhalla*, just to give you an idea. Tiny gardens, leaded windows, creosoted fencing. Crinkly curtains. Rotating washing lines, and nowhere to stand when you're pegging out, except in the mud. I do find that a bind, but ours is ever such a nice place! We only had the one day to come down and sort things out. The estate agents gave us a map and we drove out here, following the trail. To the world's end it seemed. Hurrp! 'N I said to Phil, hey, this is an adventure! We're like a couple of frontier persons, aren't we? But he's never gone much on American classics, Philip. He's more of a *Treasure Island* man than anything else.

Everything did seem rather flat and windy. We found out later that most of the land had been reclaimed from the sea, which means there's always this vast blankness overhead. The sky, and nothing between eye and sky, except the land, ever so damp and flat in front of us. Of course it does have possibilities. Given the right sort of marketing I reckon the place could become a paradise for people who still believe the earth is really flat, hurrp!

There were quite a lot of houses up for sale, but there was only the one we could afford. We drew up outside and we were just getting ourselves sorted, when a woman opened her bedroom window and shouted, It's gorn! Uxcuse me, it's gorn! But that one over there — and she pointed, is up for sale. So we trotted over the way and saw a young man, late twenties. Very eager to sell. Told us he'd just been offered an engineering job in Abu Dhabi. He was ever so keen. So there it was, all done in a day. We felt pleased with ourselves. Knocked him down a quid or two. Hurrp! But he was quite willing. Wanted to be off.

I asked him about his post, I said, but what about your post, you'll want us to send it on? And he said, Oh just pass it over the fence to the girl next-door, she'll do the honours. So that was what we did. And the first time, she took a bundle and didn't say anything. (Divorcée, early thirties, I should think.) But the second time we knocked, she refused point blank. Said she didn't see why she should have to deal with it. And Philip said but what about this poor chap, waiting for his mail in Abu Dhabi? She just looked at us as though we were mad. Abu Dhabi? He's gone back to his parents in Abertridwr, she said. Only a couple of miles up the motorway, apparently. So there it was. Though I could see why she didn't want to be bothered. He hadn't cleared his debts, had he? Little catalogues and things, various items.

New home owners, they get you to buy. Gadgets and installations, stuff you don't need. Take this lounge for instance. It was riddled with spotlights, up and down the walls, all over the ceiling. Everywhere. The young man was ever so proud of them. He kept flicking the switches on and off for us. 'N Philip stood behind me and muttered, Flashing lights? Thank God neither of us is a migraine sufferer, eh, Dodo? Hurrp! We could see he thought they were a selling point. A feature, as they say. Of course, once we moved in, we had to spend the first few weeks wandering around with tubs of filler in our hands, filling up the holes — because he ripped the spotlights out and took them with him, in the end, didn't he? Thought he'd put one over on us too, I should imagine, hurrp!

Still, it was a good move. This was the only place where we had any roots to speak of (Philip's sister, Rosemarie, who's a bit of prickly cactus, but still). It's amazing how everything has gradually spread out in the years we've been away. And I do like living here, even though the neighbours aren't what you'd call terribly 'neighbourly'. Which is what the Crime Prevention Officer said to Philip when he gave the place the once over. Another marvellous invention, Crime Prevention Officers; they give their advice free! Though what he actually said was, nobody reports anything suspicious any more. 'N I said to Philip, well I expect they're all out at work, scrabbling to pay their mortgages, aren't they? (This was before Philip landed the little office job during the day; it was when he was driving the ice-cream van, nights.)

Anyway, two burglaries in two weeks, both of them on our side of the estate. The Crime Prevention chap seemed to put some of the blame on the people themselves. Oh you should be alright, Mr Dryden, he said, looking round. It's all videos 'n' flat screen tellys these days. Gold taps in the bathrooms, microwave ovens an' that type of carry on. So there you have it. We did put a double lock on the bedroom door though, just in case. Lock ourselves in and let them get on with it, eh?

Which reminds me, I'll have to set Percival up in the kitchen before I do venture out. Philip normally does it, but he went off in a sulk. He gets the most terrific sulks! I blame some of it on the car; we had to sell the car when we made the move. But now we've both got jobs of a sort, he thinks it'd be a good idea for us to go out and buy a motor-bike for him to ride back and fore to work on; and me ride pillion. He was furious when I told him I didn't want to ride pillion any more. I said, Philip, I know I've done it in the past — (the dim and distant past, when we did our courting) but I'm fifty-nine years old now, I've got leaky veins; I'm a bum steer! I thought that'd make him laugh, the reference to my posterior but — fat chance. I didn't dare let on about its being dangerous for a sixty-four-year-old. Much too hurtful, because he was a good biker, years ago. I remember him riding his father's Harley Davidson (a World War I effort) straight through a bonfire one Guy Fawkes night, then turning his head to see if I'd noticed. And of course I had! We were nineteen and twenty-four then. Note the five year gap between our ages? That meant that we were just right for each other, our immaturities matched.

Of course, mother witheld her approval. Not that I took much notice of what she thought... It was Ma who brought me up, as one of her own almost, even though she got paid for it. But I mustn't start in on that tack, it's too early in the day for it.

Where's Piddles? Gone out already? Good. I'll just get Percy sorted in the kitchen and I'll be off myself.

Now then Percival... let me just see if I can sit you down here, like that. Whoops! Not sideways, you mustn't slump sideways. Don't want them thinking you're a collapsed alcoholic, do we? That's better... Did you know that ninety-nine per cent of all crime is opportunist. Ninety-nine point *nine* per cent for burglaries. That's what the C.P.O. chap said. So the only answer is to keep them guessing, raise that little bit of uncertainty in their minds whenever you can. Which is why we've dug Percy out of the ottoman (he's a bolster, really). Very broad and bulky. Looks like a human body. Propped up on the high-backed stool. Pity he's striped of course. That woven twill. Used to make everything with navy-blue stripes in those days didn't they? Bedding I mean. Very utilitarian. Still, that can be sorted... I'll just bring this pink pillow-slip down over the top half... just enough to cover... It's for the face, mainly. And there we are...

Flesh tones. An unhealthy shade of coral pink perhaps, but it'll do. You'd be surprised, how people only ever take in a general impression. I saw a science programme once, on television. They made this man walk round a university campus all day long, with a black plastic bin-liner over his head. When they questioned the students afterwards, most of them said they'd seen a black *man* wandering about. Probably thought he was suffering from melt down or something, hurrp!

Students, eh? Of course, the ones I work for are a nice enough bunch. But they often get my dander up in supermarkets. (I'm tying the bolster now with a bit of twine... to make the head. Use a tight knot.) Yes, have you ever stood behind them in the queue at Tesco's, students? I mean, there they are, standing two to a basket and hardly anything in it — a tin of ratatouille perhaps, a flavour-sealed pack of brie — so you think they're going to be quick... and what happens? As soon as the girl rings up the blessed total — out comes the cheque book. In sl..ow, sl..ow motion. Or the cash-card. For stuff that will hardly fill their bum bags!

And then of course, if it's a cheque they're writing they need to be told what date it is 'n who to make it out to. I want to yell: Tesco's Superstore Ltd!... honestly. It's quicker to stand behind a single mother with a trolley full of kids.... Because I'll tell you one thing, about the *really* less well off — they have to pay cash... just pulling the zipper on the lumber jacket, now. Mustn't forget to turn the collar up, macho-style... There, he really looks... I mean from a distance... Of course he's legless, but they're not gunna notice that... it's only a waist-up effect we're after. I'm rather enjoying this, I am. I'll just prop this newspaper in front of the teapot. It's a bit tricky... you need just the right amount of... but it definitely adds to the overall effect. Don't you think?

Philip's never thought of adding a newspaper. That's my own idea, my artistic flair coming to the fore. Because of the new job perhaps? Though maybe it was there already. After all, I have spent most of my working life helping customers create an illusion.

72

Ladies fashion, all the big name shops... or the more exclusive, smaller establishments. My last position was at de Valois' which was very select. Miss de Valois herself came and said a few words when I was leaving. Dorothy, she said, and she shook my hand. You're a *damn* fine saleswoman. And you're only half as neurotic as when you first came here. That was what she said, 'n I was ever so pleased about that.

Now then, are we all set? Must remember to leave these sliding doors wide open... let them see straight through to the kitchen where Percy'll be hunkered over the breakfast bar, deep in last night's Echo. Toodle-loo Percy. Bye!

I wasn't gone long, was I? Not long... exactly, but you know how time flies when you're going round the supermarket working out the pros and cons. Special offer: twelve little batter puddings, Yorkshire's in a twin-pack. Only ten pence off but how much d'you save on batter? 'N gas? It's a lot to think about, when you're wheeling your trolley round... But what was I thinking when I finally got home and stood on the doorstep, turning the key in the lock? Well, nothing really. My mind was a blank. A complete blank.

Which was what I told the policeman when he tried to get me to remember. The two bags were heavy. I'd dragged them half-way into the hall, before I even noticed — through the lounge doors our little foot-stool, lying on the carpet with its legs in the air. Then I saw the state on the bureau. All the drawers hanging open. And untidy handfuls of things, old letters and bills and insurance policies, had all been turned over and left to fall, piece-meal to the floor. I dumped the bags and rushed upstairs. Pulled back the mattress — 'n our bundle of notes was missing.

Of course, I called the police. My hands were shaking as I dialled the number, 999. I thought about phoning Philip's office, but it was a bit dodgy. He's only been there about a month, 'n we still haven't worked it out — about personal phone calls for the office junior, which is what he says he is most of the time. Anyway, what could he do at a distance? The police were very good, they sent someone round immediately.

No forced entry? We were standing in the kitchen and I could see his eyes going from the windows, which were shut, to the door which was bolted, top and bottom. Then his eyes went back to the windows. Well, everything seems secure — he strode across to the sink, and lifted the curtain. Had to bend his head a bit, to see out. Does anyone in your family ride a motor-bike? he asked.

I was flummoxed, but he unbolted the back door and showed me the tyre marks, deep in the mud. And the footprints, more than one pair, according to him. They brought it round the side look, parked it here and just — wheeled it away again. I started to say something about the bike being used for a quick get-away of course, but he didn't let me finish. Might be an idea to phone your husband, he said. I mean, whoever took that money used a front door key, don't you think?

When I came off the phone to Philip, I was miserable with embarrassment, and full of apologies. I am sorry, I said. I really am most terribly sorry, officer. Dragging you out on a wild goose chase —

So you haven't been burgled?

No, I said. I'm afraid we haven't —

Of course, I gave him the details, made a clean breast of it. I said, you see, what's happened is, my husband's gone and bought a Honda from a twenty-year-old who works in his office. They gave it a trial run — it's only five minutes along the motorway according to Philip — from their office to here. So it's a saving really, in travelling time. Naturally he wanted me to see it first, before he made an offer, this being my day off and everything, but I was out you see, shopping at Tesco's —

To give him his due, he was quite nice about it, this policeman. Said he was glad it was sorted, that was the main thing. Then he brought out his notebook and asked a few more questions... They always do that, don't they, the police? Before they let you off the hook. I was going on alright until I saw him eyeing Percy in the corner. It was all he could do to keep a straight face... I felt about *this* high. Then he went through a whole string of questions, wanting to know where I worked, where Philip worked, how long we've been living here and so on. There didn't seem any point, but he wrote it all down. To put us on computer somewhere, I expect.

By the time I saw him out, I was thoroughly depressed. I took two portions of ice-cream from the fridge and ate them both. Then I went upstairs to have a lie down. Picked up *Little Lord Fauntleroy*, but I couldn't get past that little face on the cover. Those sickening yellow ringlets down to his shoulders. So girlish. Reminded me of myself when I was that age. Sickening. Running home from Sunday-school in a new candy-striped frock, with a straw hat on the back of my head, shouting Yoo-hoo! Ma, love, yoo-hoo! (I knew there were bound to be visitors in the best room) I was a *terrible* little show-off in those days. I was really... always on the look-out for attention. 'N I remember this strange woman jumping to her feet and shouting at me as I twirled round in front of Ma. That is not your ma-ther! *That* is *not* your ma-ther! She kept shouting it at me until I stopped twirling. *I* am your ma-ther she said, 'n look at you, got up like some tupenny ha'penny little floosie. Of course, I'd no idea about father being off somewhere in the army... the both of them. I *loved* Ma... I'd no idea.

Ridiculous. Sniffling over something that must have happened all of fifty years ago... but I can't help it. Especially after today. I mean, look at us. We're like a couple of kids, Philip and myself — which is what I told the girl behind the desk at the Job Centre, when she asked my age. I said, I'm fifty-nine years old, and my husband Philip is sixty-four, but you'd never think it. She seemed quite taken with the five year gap between our ages. That's clever she said, that means you're finishing your working lives in tandem! Very important. Pension wise.

Nice girl, I could see her point. Then I said, but what about the next eleven months? We both need to find work. You see, my husband's spent the last thirty years or so, really getting stuck into Kalamazoo, the salaries 'n wages system? I mean really getting stuck in. He knows it inside out, he's an expert... but what's happened is, his firm's thrown in the towel 'n gone over to computer base, and Philip's been left high and dry — d'you follow? She said, yes she did follow, and held up both her hands as if to say, spare me the details. But I thought I'd better explain a little further: of course we knew we had to get out, I said. 'N get on our bikes. We could see that. No use sitting out the extra year, otherwise we'd never have been able to afford the move, what with house prices 'n so on. But when we got here, of course, we found out that having used our initiative 'n quit work off our own bats, neither of us was entitled to any dole money. 'N we've had terrible trouble ever since... trying to find jobs 'n —

She did interrupt me then because she'd had enough. Asked me what type of work I was looking for? Oh, anything! I said. Anything at all! (Only no standing, I thought to myself. Please God, no standing, because of the leaky veins.) Just as well I kept my mouth shut on that last point. Said they were looking for someone to model at the College of Art & Design. A model? I couldn't help being thrilled. I think it was the 'art and design' bit that did for me. She picked a card, dialled a number 'n got me an interview for that very afternoon. Threw me into a tiz. I had to rush over to Philip's sister Rosemarie's 'n practically beg her to lend me the little mustard yellow jacket to wear with my tailored slacks. What for? You're over fifty-five, Dorothy, people over fifty-five *never* get taken on. It says in the paper... Anyway, she did lend it me (though I must say mustard yellow's too vibrant a colour for Rosemarie, she should stick to pastels). Perhaps it made an impression... the bods in the fine art department offered me the job on the spot. Modelling in the nud. Said they were desperate to find a well rounded figure, flesh that looked as if it'd been lived in. Hurrp!

Philip was not too keen. Kept looking at me strangely. But how do you feel about it? he kept asking. In yourself? Well, how d'you cope with a male-ego interrogation question like that eh? Except with a bit of unglamorous truth. I mean to say, posing's a killer — Can you arch your spine 'n throw your head back Dorothy, and hold it there, just for three minutes — 'N so *boring*, you've no idea. The rates of pay aren't bad, though. Much higher than I'd get for being a kitchen help... Where I slipped up was in telling him I was allowed to lie down. In between poses, wrapped in my dressing-gown of course, but sent him off the deep end for some reason... the idea of me having a rest, in between poses... Just as I'm doing now on this bed, on my day off. Gathering my strength.

Out like a light 'til he woke me up at six. Eat up, he said, you're looking a bit peaky. He'd gone and made me a great big meal hadn't he? Cabbage, Yorkshires, roasters... and a raspberry fool for afters. Hmmmm. There's a card here for you too, he said, as I ate my way through. And a box of chocolates. Oh? Picked up the card 'n had a look 'Well done Dodo, for doing your bit'. I looked at that card for a long time, chewing, thinking. Is it alright then? he said, as I downed the last mouthful. 'S alright, I said. Meat could've done a bit longer... Then I said oh, come on then. Let's go and have a dekko at it. The motorbike. It was surprising, how nice and shiny it looked looming out of the darkness around the back. Of course, we ended up taking a quick spin into town. Flying down the motor-way at a steady knot. No Percy in the kitchen though — I was wearing his lumber jacket and the rest of him was stuffed inside the closet. This jacket's quite a jazzy one. Saw it in a shop window one day 'n I thought, that's a bit jazzy! Hang on girl, I'll bet they don't shift that. And they didn't, not for the asking price. I felt quite chirpy with it on. Got quite a few startled glances, from families in their cars.

When we got in to town, we went straight to the amusement arcade didn't we? Made a bee-line for the slot-machines I did. The female attendant was round the same age as me, pushing sixty I should say. Poor dear kept coming up and offering me these tokens, for so much off at the supermarket. Made me ever so cross, she was spoiling my concentration! Wanting to chat... in the end I said, look, I hope you don't mind, but I'm trying to

win this jackpot. She started to move away from me then, and I
found myself shouting after her. No, sorry, honestly, but it's great
fun... you should try it. *We* enjoy it. Tremendously... I could see
Philip over the far side playing his space-invader machine like a
mad thing. We're like a couple of kids, I shouted. The pair of
us...

MOONBEAM KISSES

The day after the Pope died they put me in an orphanage, which they said was a 'home'. Fair enough. But I fell asleep in the car, and when we got there, all I could hear was this voice saying: 'Welcome to the Home of St Michael and All the Archangels.' Well, I was only nine and although I threw my head back as far as I could, the stone letters over the archway were so tangled up with thorns and leaves and fat white roses that I couldn't make out what they said. Then I saw the nun, kneeling on the path with a trowel in her hands, and I thought I must have died and gone to heaven. Except that I knew, no girl like me would go there.

The nun with the trowel was Sister Mary John. When she stood up, she shook out the black sleeves of her habit like great bat wings and stamped her feet hard so that the loose earth fell over the crazy paving. She wore black Wellington boots with the tops turned down like a worky, and she did not smile as she looked at me and said, 'What is it they call you? What?' I told her my name and she grunted. Behind the nun was a stone-rimmed fountain with a statue of Our Lady in the middle of it. Water sprayed up in front of Her outstretched hands, while the first toe of Her right foot flattened the head of a snake completely.

Inside the house, which was tall with windows arched like a church, a small nun with red cheeks smiled and flipped a hand at the bun on top of my head. 'It's Margaret-Rose isn't it? Well, Margaret-Rose, we'll have to get rid of this muff, won't we?' She slapped my hair again and I seemed to see the dust motes whizz around my head like some shameful halo. 'Yes, Sister.'

'Yes,' she clamped her mouth and nodded, 'but it's bath first, then something to eat and then we'll get the pinking shears out!'

By early evening I was tucked up in bed, just like the children in the picture books, and before the curtains were drawn, I lay inside my wide striped sheets and watched the clouds in glory. First they were yellow and pale like gold, then red like lolly ice with the colouring almost sucked out. My head felt small against the pillow and as I watched the rain clouds seep across, I could feel the silver clippers on the back of my neck and hear the nuns crying 'Shorn! Shorn! Shriven!' as the hair came away in clumps. After it was all off they threw it onto the fire where it raised a white wispy smoke that stank.

At St. Michael and All the Archangels I was happy for a time. I had a name, Margaret-Rose, and a parentage that put me down in the gold coloured ledgers as 'half-caste'. I knew that this meant me, my arms, my legs, my head, my body. Me. But I did not *understand* until that first evening, when I stood in the darkness of the vestry and dipped my fingers into the tepid waters of the font. Then the words came back into my head and stayed. 'Half-caste' — like the grainy metal surface of the bowl. Greeny-bronze, like metal, half-caste. Later, when groups of children came up to me in the playground and asked if I was from Africa, I shook my head and smiled to reassure them.

Every morning after prayers the nuns gave out milk from a crate, one half-bottle to each child. And we handled the thick cold glass lovingly, walling our eyes on the table-mats in front of us and sucking up the milk through waxed straws, right down to the last trickle. After milk, the nuns asked us questions from the pale blue catechism book.

'Margaret-Rose, who made you? In whose image and likeness were you made?' As soon as Sister repeated the question I became confused. All I could think of was the song playing in Mrs Edwards' house. Sister smiled at me as if she knew the song. And I could hear it playing loudly in my head, the one about 'too many moonbeam kisses, too many sunbeams cooling' and Duggie's voice leaning over me all the time saying, 'I bet you doan know, I bet you doan know...' Sister waited and waited for me to speak, then she waved her hand and turned to Claire Tumelty.

Claire Tumelty had eyes like glass alleys and dark, curled hair. She wore pastel coloured skirts with the pleats as rigid as the pleats on a sea-shell; and she did not eat mashed potatoes or drink milk, because she was allergic. Now she sat very still with her hands folded, waiting for Sister to repeat the question. 'Claire, who made you?' And she answered quietly, 'God, God made me.' And Sister said, 'Yes, that's it, that's what I was after,' and turned the page.

I never knew the difference between what I was supposed to know and what I was not supposed to know. Though I sensed that girls like Claire Tumelty always did. She was at St Michael's because her mother was ill, while I had been put there for being 'too knowing'. I remember my foster mother, Mrs Edwards, unwinding the spotted flex from the electric iron and telling the visitor as she plugged it in to the wall, that Margaret-Rose was 'knowing, awfully *knowing* for a kiddy as young as she is.' Then she had sighed and said, 'My own were never like it, never.' I left the room and waited on top of the landing until the visitor had gone. When Mrs Edwards called me down I was afraid of what she was going to say, but she only asked me to go to the shops and went on ironing a pile of clothes, including Duggie's vest and things.

That was the evening the Pope died. It was still light when I opened the side-door to put the bottles out. People were burning leaves and rubbish in their gardens and I could smell the smoke as Duggie wheeled his bike in. 'Your old fella's dead then,' he said and laughed. 'Give you something to talk about when you gets to the nuns, woan it?' I had smiled and nodded, though I didn't understand. His eyes glittered like the pieces of coal in the coal-house; and I wondered if it was raining, though I knew that it was not.

The next day I had sat in the back-seat of the car with a vanity-case on my lap and looked at the sky while Duggie and his girl-friend sat on the bumpy red leather seat of his motor-bike and waited for me to go. The sky was white with thin blue cracks in it like ice floes. I closed my eyes and opened them. Nothing moved. It was as if the world had stopped moving. Duggie's hair was black and shiny with brylcreem, and the girl-friend wore a bri-nylon top with ice-blue stripes. I watched as she tied a red chiffon scarf around her head. I did not know what she was called because she was new, but when the car pulled out and they zoomed in front of us, I saw that they were both wearing dark glasses and she was holding on, tightly.

Nobody ever told me that roses were a symbol of love, and it wasn't something you could tell just by looking. At St Michael and All the Archangels, the nuns had created a 'Garden of Roses For the Blind'. The roses were all white or cream or the very darkest red, and money and silver paper had been collected to pay for them. On Saturday afternoons most of the children went home, but I was told to go and help Sister in the garden.

At first I thought I had been specially chosen, though I didn't know why. The rich knots of colour embedded in the bushes confused me, while the faint perfume from the single stems gave me a headache. Sister Mary John hardly spoke except to shout 'Mind your feet' or 'Hand me the secateurs — the secateurs!' Yet she showed me how to water all the plants in the green house and how to place the big old fashioned records on the small white plastic record player in the corner. *Where E'er You Walk* and *Now Sleeps the Crimson Petal* were the ones she wanted to hear as she tended the blossoms.

It became my task to keep the records playing. And while they played, I stood quietly in the doorway of the green-house looking out across the garden. From where I was standing I could see the back of Our Lady's head, all grey and crumbly with holes like leprosy; and next to her the black and white figure of Sister Mary John, kneeling on the gravel path, mulching the roses. As I watched, the hiss and crackle of the record mingled with the sounds of the water falling from the fountain and made my heart sad.

82

'Double blossoms are made in heaven, Margaret-Rose, where are they made?'

'Heaven, Sister.'

'Yes. But you see, the creation of great beauty involves unpleasantness. Always. That is why I seldom wear gloves.' She held out her hands. They were stained and evil smelling where she had smeared and patted the mounds of compost around each stem. I moved my head and she showed her teeth in a smile. 'Don't be afraid of the smell Margaret-Rose, the smell won't hurt you. Decayed leaf and vegetable matter, that's all it is.' The amusement in her voice made me feel small; and at the end of the afternoon she remembered it again: 'Oh Margaret-Rose is heaving / Over leaf-mould smells a-seething, ha! Do you know any poetry?' 'No sister.' 'No!' Her laugh was like a bark and I walked along beside her not knowing what to say. Before we went inside, I asked her quietly if it was a priest who sang on the records, but she said no, it was an Irish tenor.

The time I spent at St. Michael's is concertinaed in my mind, with the memories packed up tight or drawn out slowly like a sigh. A week after I arrived, we sat in the main hall and watched the Pope being buried on television. They carried him out on a bier, face up with his hands crossed. His vestments were crimson and gold and he looked like a Punch and Judy man, with the rosy patches on his waxy cheeks and his enormous nose jutting out against the bright blue sky. While we were watching, Claire Tumelty leaned across and asked if she could borrow my vanity case for the week-end. I said no.

Everything is scrunched up in my mind. We said a *De Profundis* for the dead Pope and prayed that perpetual light would shine upon him. Later we were brought into the hall again to watch the new Pope being elected. The building they showed looked just like the children's clinic across the road from Mrs Edwards' house. I imagined all the cardinals sat inside, waiting for their new father. When the white smoke rose from the chimney and the voice sounded out like a prayer: *'Habemoum Papos'*, the nuns all clapped their hands and smiled. Claire Tumelty turned around in her chair to face me and I got ready to say no again. But this time she just looked at me and said, 'How come you never go home on a Saturday, Margaret-Rose? Doesn't anybody want you?'

Afterwards they said I was jealous. Jealous because I hadn't been chosen as a flower-girl. Claire Tumelty was chosen. There were five of them altogether, in long white dresses and pale green satin cloaks. Sister said they looked like angels, with the fresh flowers in their hair and the baskets of petals over their arms. What they had to do was walk in formation — raise a handful of petals to their lips, then turn and scatter them at the feet of the Archbishop walking behind. The ceremony was for the new Pope and in remembrance of the old. The procession should have wound its way through the Garden of Roses for the Blind, but it all took place on the front lawn instead, because of my destructiveness.

I was thinking about the blind as I stood quietly in the garden and tore the roses from their stems. It was night-time and the sky was dark blue like the blue of a Milk of Magnesia bottle. It shaded out the white and the cream and the red of the roses, so that the whole garden looked like an engraving, with everything grey or black. My hands were full of roses. I thought about perpetual light and perpetual darkness as I ripped and tore at the fattest ones. It was the feel of the soft skinned petals falling. They filled my hands and I flung them down. I was sure my eyes looked black. I thought of the black metal box, the meter box, high on the wall in Mrs Edwards' house. Perpetual light and perpetual darkness. When the light went out you had to find your way in the dark. It took ages. Then you reached up and dropped two silver coins in the slot. The light came back on and people slapped your face. Slapped your face and shouted. Shouted.

By the time I came to, I had stripped the garden of over half its roses. Some of the heads lay whole on the gravel path, but a lot of the petals had been dismembered. Sister Mary John slapped me hard across both cheeks and said, 'Lower your brazen face'.

My skin felt brazen, hot like metal before it cools, brazen as brass. Then the feeling went, and I stood still as a statue with my head bowed, while two other nuns led her away. I heard them talking about 'a garden lover'; 'a garden lover and a truss of roses'.

The ceremony took place the afternoon before I left. I was put at the back with some of the older girls. They laughed and patted me on the shoulder, and asked me where I was being sent. The sky was white and heavy and it looked as though it was going to rain. After the ceremony, the Archbishop came over to talk to us. Then he blessed us with the sign of the cross and turned to go, but the older girls kept grabbing his hands and shouting 'Father! Father!' laughing up at his face all the while. The nuns tried to move him away gently, but the girls wouldn't let them. They made it into a joke. And the Archbishop went on smiling and trying to claim his hands back. He was dribbling slightly from the corner of his mouth, where he'd had a stroke.

BLESSED TIMES FOR A
BLACKY GROCER

June 12th, 1780. On this day I got up only to fall down behind
the little wicket gate at the entrance to my shop. Two or three
pieces of fruit tumbled down around my head also. How long did
I lie there? I do not know. But when I came to? Gracious God!
Behold my transformation.

Like a turtle laid out upon its back, I could not move, except to
make amphibious motion with the two small arms that flapped
against the monstrous swelling of my gut. Amidst this darkness,
there was a sound as of rushing waters, that swept against the
shell of my back and carried on past my head where it seemed to
die in gentle plash. Plash. By the bye my attention was taken
with the pieces of fruit that had fallen beside me, two lemons
and one lime, all of which seemed to glow with unearthly
phosphorescence in the dimness of that shop.

Oh bitter fruits! The sands of time! Born on a slave ship in
the mid-Atlantic, my mother died, my father killed himself—
but how to recount Life's History without a self pitying tear or
two? My eyeballs bulge, my tongue distends — nothing! Perhaps
it is a tale grown stale with the telling, at any rate, it fails to
crank the engines of my heart. But stay, the shutters are going
up, the bright light stabs my eye like lemon on oyster and Anne,
my fine black lady, stands in the doorway, contemplating me
thus.

'Sancho?'

'Oh Mrs Sancho! dearest, you must bury me like a Hindoostan,
yes, send me out to sea, just as the orange glow of the sun slips
down behind the Thames at Greenwich — ' I cough, I snuffle, I

catch my breath and my eyes! Oh miracle, my eyes are pearled with tears and I am speechless.

'Sancho?' She has marched around my body with a heavy tread, her voice is low her face looms over mine. 'Man-beast, old pee-bag, you have emptied your bladder, Sir, upon the floor which is almost completely awash. Why the sawdust itself is sodden, it will take an hour at the least to cleanse this place and you!'

'Bladder, bladder, bladder, blather...'

Her eyes become fixed on the shelf behind my head, she springs forward. 'Merciful heavens, can it be? Why we are completely out of rice and green tea both!'

I roll my head back and forth in an agony of emotion, the shop! the shop! the detestable comestibles! My voice comes back: 'I am dying, Egypt, dying.' At this she turns, and briskly taking up my hand, kneels down beside my body. 'You are not dying, Ignatius Sancho... you have the old man's weakness is all. Come, let me pop some sugar into your mouth, it will sweeten your thoughts as well as give you strength.'

My Mrs Sancho! So young in years, and yet so firm of purpose. And such solidity of aspect! Why she is positively pyramidal — she whose form I once likened to the finest sifting of black gold sand...

Let me down gently, *gently*, ouf! I am a fat old fellow I know. Ah me, Mary, Fanny, Betsy, Lydia, Kitty — and my dear wife. God bless my sanchonettas. And Billy, where is he? Hidden under an armpit! Come forth my little sanchonet; and do you take up this fan and stir the air about my face. Ah, performed to perfection, my very own little *black boy* — such great sad eyes and butter-ball shape, he is the image of my younger self. But see here Betsy, while I think on it, run and fetch the paring knife to take away this hard skin from my feet... No grimacing my dear, I'll warrant it will come away like cheese rind... Oh that I may show this sinful world a clean pair of heels...

But I did not die that month, that flaming month, yet have instead continued much the same, except that I have taken permanently to my bed. The physician, who is not much good, puts it down to age (I am at least fifty-one years old); to corpulence (fifty-one again); and to an overly sensitive reaction to the activities of the mob — my collapse coming as it did only days after the riots led by my Lord George Gordon. Crowds running amok, streets turned into burning lakes — the vulpine faces pressing in on ours — enough! It frightens me to think of it. My dear wife now runs the shop, together with the help of my children; and very able they all are too.

As for me, my mind is becoming more and more obsessed with that mysterious coincidence of place and person in my life. The primary example being 'Blackamore' and 'Blackheath', where my late patron, Lord Montagu, lived. *'Blackamore'* and *'Blackheath'* — think on it — but first, regard the lilies of the field. In this instance, the Misses F at Greenwich, who owned me from the age of two. These three ladies put a turban on my head and a big kettle over my arm, before they named me 'Sancho' after that eternal servant in *Don Quixote*.

'Sancho?'

'Sancho!'

'Sancho. How very apt.'

Did my name determine my position in life? Did my position in life determine my name? In my green youth I would have answered 'Yes' to the second and 'No', a thousand times 'No!' to the first. But of late my thinking has become more circular.

I had already been christened once, on the slave ship at Cartagena, where a catholic bishop boarded the ship and baptised every male one of us — every slave that is — 'Ignatius' and every female — I know not what. My three white ladies, who got the tale from a nephew captain, were silent on this. Nevertheless, in accordance with papist doctrine, we were now entitled to die and go straight to heaven, thus circumventing altogether the hapless state of limbo.

Perhaps I did die then? And in dying prove the emptiness of Romish ritual. For by the time I came to a consciousness of myself as Ignatius Sancho, the Misses F's little black at Greenwich, I found to my astonishment that I had been living in limbo for some time.

> I looked at the moon
> on the back of a spoon,
> and a secret I will tell thee
> that the man in the moon,
> on the back of a spoon,
> is never a he! but a she!
> With one face divided by three.

Dear ladies, sweet white ladies, oh the salt and sugar of them! as they chucked me under the chin, and curled my feather tight – so tight. Laughing as they dropped the folded notes onto my tea-tray, calling me their little black cherub and sending me out – hither and thither on those endless errands of love. Though they were all three of them well over the age of five and thirty!

Ah well, I would not begrudge them that, not that. And I did learn my letters through waiting on them at the card-table, peeping over their shoulders and calling out. At first they even encouraged me in this showing off, for it was a great source of wonderment among the company to see a little blackamore perform such tricks. It also brought me to the attention of my Lord Montagu, who banged me on the noddle and charged each one of the Misses F with the sacred duty to cultivate such hopeful soil.

My dear wife enters the room at this point and bustles about, filling the jugs and emptying the slop-bowl. She pauses long enough to inform me that Nollekins the sculptor visited the shop this morning to ask about my health; and that Mr Samuel Johnson's man-servant came this afternoon to enquire about the same. I nod my head happily, so many callers! So many enquiries after my well-being!

'Not one of them bought anything.' My wife is standing at the foot of the bed; and as she speaks, she picks up a handful of the yellow maize or Indian corn from her pocket and works the grains between her fingers like worry-beads.

I shake my head and try to explain. She remains obdurate: 'Not a half a candle or an ounce of flour between them.'

'But my dear Anne, such great friendship as theirs is —'

'Friendship? I would not call that *friendship*!' She flings out a hand and the golden grains scatter about my head like buckshot. My eyes blink, but in an instant she is there, kneeling at my side to calm my fears. I attempt to take her hand but she shakes me off, says she has come to pick up the grains that have fallen down behind the bed post. Did I mention by the bye, that my wife is a most meticulous and thrifty person?

Now lifting her head from her task, she regards me with a cold eye. 'You and your endless *hob-nobbing*! Have you not spent a lifetime at it? Taking a dish of tea with this one, and a glass of wine with that one —' suddenly she twists up her mouth, disturbing the smooth black cast of her features. Her voice takes on a puling, obsequious, sycophantic note, wherein I recognise some monstrous caricature of myself — albeit overlaid with the accents of our West Indies: 'Oh ah mos write me a letter to me good friend Mister Garrick, Mister Johnson, or the Rev'rend Mister Sterne, Sir, Mister Laurence Sterne... Me good friends, all me good friends, me *good*, *good*, friends nah!'

I close my eyes in despair. Oh that my dear wife had a better understanding of the ways of this world! Though in truth she is a woman of quick parts, extremely quick — can tell at a glance how many strawberries there are piled in one basket; how many seeds sewn into a pomegranate — how many feathers even are hanging from the chicken's arse before she has plucked it! Yet she has no — understanding.

I open my eyes to find her hovering directly over the bed, arms akimbo. She carries the mark of slavery on her upper arm, where the round O has been cut out, not burned into the flesh; the flap being filled with ashes, so that the raised skin has grown over it. To my tired eyes, it has the sheen of battered metal, like an amulet, rising and falling with her words as she demands to know who it is I think I am?

'Why, my love,' say I, perplexed, 'I am a one-time butler to my Lord Montagu... now laid upon his pillows like a lord himself!' At last she begins to smile and I find myself restored to sudden favour. She descends the stairs with cheerful step, leaving me to fester with my thoughts.

They float, the lilies float, though their stems have rooted in my guts. I feel them now, pulling against the gaseous air that bloats up the body of this jolly, coal-black African...

Did I mention that I was once a cherub? Yes? Alas, I grew too big. My three white ladies pushed me from their laps, banished me to a downstairs kitchen and bade me make myself useful. Useful! I laid down upon my pallet and refused to budge. Then it was they came to me — with honeyed words and smart slaps — all to no avail. Until at last they threw up their hands and declared themselves defeated. I had won, they said, and they would therefore be making arrangements for me to travel out to the West Indies forthwith, where I would take up a position as an *Assistant Planter*, no less.

My astonishment on receiving this news can scarcely be imagined. I at once threw down the anti-slavery tract I had been reading, and vowed to shoot myself in the head. Of course they denied it, all three of them denied having any intention of selling me back into slavery. But I had read Malachy Postlethwayt! and I knew that *Assistant Planter* was but the sepulchral whitening of that most horrible condition, 'Plantation Slave'.

Not long after this encounter, all my tracts and books were thrown onto the fire. They had decided to keep me on they said, but I must work, AND I MUST NOT READ!!! Having nothing to occupy my mind made me languorous. I therefore fell asleep for many hours at a stretch. Until one day my three white ladies woke me with a kick and the message to be off — the door was wide open, they said, and I was free to wander through it. London abounded with beggars — I was aware of that? Aye well, doubtless

I would soon find my way to St Giles, and there scratch out a living amongst my fellow 'Blackbirds'. For themselves they wished me no ill will — no, none at all. Adieu, adieu. Adieu.

My wife pokes her head around the door and I think to ask what day it is. 'Day?' says she, coming heavily into the room, 'Why the day is almost gone.' Then she tells me that it is half-past nine of the clock, on the thirteenth day of December, and that she has managed to salt down the hog etc. as well as to pound a goodly supply of the Indian corn — everything was well in hand for the Lenten months to come.

She is making preparations, I think dully, my wife is busy making preparations for a time ahead of mine. Before going down again, she promises she will bring me a bowl of soup, as soon as ever the corn has simmered itself to tenderness. My wife is a good woman, but Lord love us! Maize and pork stew?

I am an Englishman. 'I should prefer roast-beef,' I call out after her, 'Plum pudding, or buttered eggs even.'

Of course my teeth are long gone. I sink down into gloom, press my fingers to the corners of my mouth and, childlike, peer into the looking-glass. White stubble speckles the blackness of my underthroat and chin, and my face is small: ready for death, I think, shoving my fingers hard against my mouth and grinning savagely. The diffuse, milky-blue eyesight of old age lends my fingernails the appearance of daintily ridged, shell-like teeth. 'Sticks and feathers!' I cry out. 'Is this the African face painted by one Thomas Gainsborough in an hour and forty minutes?' Though that was not *my* face, no, not my face at all. I shake my head and peer into the looking-glass again. But now my features have seeped away entirely and I am gazing into the darkness. I throw the mirror down and cry out loud (in my most Shakespearian voice): 'Who is it that will tell me who I am?'

It was Betsy and William who came to me; and though William soon crept away, Betsy laid my head upon her lap and listened while I spoke and did not yawn, though I daresay she had heard it all before.

Of how my Lord Montagu, when visiting the sisters at Greenwich, had always encouraged my ambitions, delighting in making me presents of expensive books, and souring the faces of the sisters even further by telling them that their blackamore might well be an African Prince. Here he would pause to give a touch to the greeny-blue feathers affixed to the side of my turban — it was their duty, he would tell them sternly, to nurture such talent.

Oh my Lord Montagu! Did I tell you that he was once a Governor of the Island of Jamaica? A social and agricultural experimentalist? And a good man. He it was who held out 'Those golden lamps in a green night'.

Of course it was to Richmond that I made my way when the sisters turfed me out, only to discover that my glorious patron had died in the night! I wait for Betsy to show the requisite surprise upon her face before continuing. The Duchess was all for sending me back to Greenwich, but I stood my ground and threatened to shoot myself in the head rather than return. So wild at heart was I then! And with such a talent for histrionics! But she did not send me back; instead I was put to the opening and closing of doors, so many doors — in short, I became a butler — or was it a footman?

Here I am obliged to stop and yawn myself. It is hard for me to remember the rest. Certainly I made myself agreeable to the household. I learned to play the flute and harpsicord — John, the third Duke, and his sister Lady Betty were particularly devoted to me. The old Duchess died and I was left a small annuity — I quit my post and moved to London, determined to nurture my genius.

Yes, my genius! But where was it? I tried my hand at composing (with some small success) as well as painting (with very little success) and versifying (with no success at all). Yet all the while I felt that acting, acting was my true, my real, calling in life. Betsy perks up a little here, for of all my children, she is the one who shares my love of the theatre. We have spent many a shilling on seats at Drury Lane.

And so I tell the tale of how one night, over a pint pot Davy Garrick himself encouraged my ambitions for the stage. Only to shake his head next morning at both my 'Othello' and my 'Orinooko', explaining, as he slapped me on the back, that both parts were irredeemably spoiled by my defect of speech. My bewilderment was extreme and must have shown upon my face — for I have no defect of speech! (And you will have to agree, will you not, having listened to these ramblings for this long amount of time?) At any rate, Davy tapped his finger here, at the very base of my throat, and said 'My dear Sancho, this colouring of *Africa* in your voice...' Of course, at this point your mother would always sniff and say that in her opinion, Mr Garrick never believed that 'Othello' was as black as he was painted anyway.

But for myself, for myself — then it was that my great red pulsing heart burst into flames — before subsiding into the softest heap of ashes this side of hell! Here Betsy nods her head, and in a dreamy voice reminds me of how the mob last summer had tried to destroy an Italian painting of Our Saviour — casting it into the deepest part of the bonfire where it had refused to burn, except for the painted flames around His Heart, which outshone, in their brightness, the raging flames of destruction.

On this miraculous image I fall asleep and dream that I have gambled away all my clothes in a game of cribbage, until at last only one large playing card stands between me and my nakedness. Of course I play the card, certain that it holds the heart shaped ace on its front. Alas it does not, it is only a child's alphabetical 'A', and I find myself naked as a babe facing the whoops and hollers of the mob.

I open my eyes to find my wife standing over the bed. She has threaded a white flower through the hole in her ear. She is smiling and serene as she plumps up the bolsters, telling me that the deterioration in my condition is entirely of my own making. 'For you have drunk too much green tea and chocolate in your life, smoked too many rolls of tobacco, crumbled too much sugar into too many carafes of wine, in short...'

Her voice travels on and for some reason I am reminded of the evening we went by water to the Vauxhall Pleasure Gardens. Like black marble statues, we sat majestically upon the dirty sacking where the bargeman had placed us. Staring straight ahead of us, ignoring the faces that flared into view and out again, and the abuse that continued to hang in the air long after we had sailed past. Coming back, we took the coach.

And now the smell of boiling laundry fills my nostrils and I enquire whether my winding sheet is being got ready? But my wife answers no, it is only the smell of the corn soup boiling down. Her voice stops, hesitates, and then continues. I scarcely attend, for the sudden blue of night has filled my vision. And Oh! melancholy fate! I am dying to the silvery tinkle of the shop-bell, which engraves itself on the darkness, as the downstairs door opens and closes.

The Gentleman's Magazine, December, 1780.
On the 14th December, in Charles Street, Westminster.
Mr Ignatius Sancho. Grocer and oilman.

Grocer and oilman indeed!

She has buried my corpse at the bottom of the garden, and in accordance with the West Indian custom, a scattering of yellow maize and a short measure of rum was poured over my blackamore head to fix the ceremony. This head is a barren, desolate spot that still waits for the green and tender shoots to sprout. But outside the blackbird sits and preens itself, crying 'Pity the brilliants! Pity the brilliants!'

ROOTS

It's June and our front garden is filled with potato plants. All spriggly leaves of deep dark green. I could curl up and die when I think of those potato plants, out there in our front like that. My father went and planted them, after Mr Blueser had dug up the ground first. Mr Blueser is a skinny, skinny man, the colour of used coin. He has wild staring eyes and he can't speak properly. He tried to say 'thank you' when I brought him a glass of water, but the veins moved up and down in his neck like pulleys, and no sound came out.

My father paid him ten shillings for the job and fed him a plate of beans and rice. He ate quickly, bulging his cheeks like Popeye and staring straight ahead of him. You could see his rib cage showing through his shirt like the inside of a rowing boat. Poor Mr Blueser. He's going home soon: the government said they'd pay his passage and send his seaman's pension out to him every three months. He dug up the garden good though; and when he'd finished raking it over, I went and stood near the edge of the concrete path and looked. The chunks of red brown earth had been crumbled into absolute evenness, you could fill your eyes with it. And no matter how hard I looked, there was nothing in that square of earth that was out of place.

How long ago was that? I hate the deadness of Sunday evenings like this. The main road is quiet: the two bus stops are empty. Every now and again, posses of stray dogs trot along the pavement, heading up, moving out. I'm fed up with this place. Everything is effing gladioli, foxgloves and box hedges, apart from next door's lavatory bowl, waiting outside their front for the council to come and collect it. And that mass of vegetation sprouting up in ours. Oh, I don't know! And how come it's Mr Blueser who's being sent away? And why has my father taken it into his head to plant potatoes out in our front for God's sake? These are questions I have to ask myself as I turn from the window in disgust.

I lie down on the bed and take one gold stud from my ear lobe. I bring my eyes up close to the ball bearing end. Pictured there, my face blazes into a kind of brightness, gold like the centre of a flower, and hedged by a couple of wintry looking bushes, artificially shaped. I am Marcia Angela Tobin, and I am fourteen years old. What does that mean? Anything? I've noticed myself becoming more and more detective, lately. I watch everyone closely. I play tape-recorded conversations in my head all the time; and I realise things.

Take my father, for instance. Lionel Tobin. At this very moment he is sat downstairs in our front room waiting for half-past seven, because he's on nights this week: and nights begin on Sundays. He'll be sitting up straight, though the settee is low and soft-cushioned. His back is always straight and his face, his working face, is dark, iron dark and unfathomable. 'Search me,' I say, using two or three different voices, 'Search me!'

He shouts my name from the foot of the stairs just before he is ready to go. I yell back, 'What!' but my feet move quickly towards the bannister, to deaden the tone of my voice. He issues instructions while counting over his bus fare. My father is a man who counts and counts — the change in his pocket, the minutes on the face of the clock. He doesn't want to miss the bus, or not have the right money. I know what he will say before he has said it. That the back door is locked eh, and to make sure you bolt this one after me, you hear? And to remember, anyone knock, you doan answer. He raises his head from his counting. 'You hear me?' I have seen the patina of his face on old coins. 'Eh?'

The door slams shut, and I wait for the clang of the gate, but his voice blasts through the letter-box to make me jump. 'Bolt this door now while I'm here.' *Me fadda always treat me like a chile, one chile, big an' stupid!* But sometimes, I think it has to do with him being a man and having to bring up a girl on his own...

I wander over to the sideboard, picking things up, putting them back down. My hands close around two glass globes, very smooth and cold. I shake them up and down like a pair of maracas. Kicking up a snow storm inside the glass blue light. Dadda brought them home from sea, when I was small, da, da. Genoa, Antwerp, Rotterdam. Three month trips. I watch the whirling snowflakes drop and settle at the bottom of each glass. Then the skies turn into clear romantic blue over beaches made of dessicated coconut. St. Vincent, Santiago, Boavista. For some reason Nat King Cole comes into my head, he wears my father's pink calypso shirt and he sings a slow song. His pro-nunciation is always demnably correct. I follow the song and shake the maracas over and over again. *'They just lie there, end. They die there... do you smile'* — Christ I'm a kid. No I am not a kid. Put them down. Get on with your work. Righto. Look, who's voice dis is? Look, the blue of the glass has tinged the browness of my one hand green...

They stare at me from their wedding photo on the mantelpiece, their doubled eyes uncomprehending. I pick up the photograph and tilt it towards the light. My father's face is mahogany, with slivers of bronze where the light falls on the left hand side of his face; the cherry red on my mother's lips is the only spot of vividness about her. I tilt the picture more sharply. Sometimes I fancy these two images are fading into the sky behind; though I keep them in my head, two faces in black and white.

Next morning, first thing, I look out through the bedroom window. I note the greenery, creeping up and up. We'll be knee deep in tuberous roots soon. As if I cared. Last night I listened to the radio until I fell asleep, and this morning I have two new songs to take to school. Once I'm there, I put on a hard face. I hate the teachers, in particular, Stanley (the ring-master) and Mary (the elephant). Break-time I go from group to group, selling cigarettes: my father's duty-free, brought by an old compadre come ashore. I'm making money. It's so easy, the way the money drops into my hand. It fascinates me. I catch bits of conversation.

'He didn't want Deniece, he wanted top.'

'She gave him top, she gave him top.'

'And bottom.'

'No, no she never, only top.'

There's a silence, then everyone laughs. It surprises me to see how hard they are, talking about a friend. I keep the surprise out of my face. I'm a black marketeer. They cluster around my packets of cigarettes. American, tipped and longer. I let them finger the gold writing on the outside of the carton.

Someone says, 'Where d'you get these from, then?' 'Stole 'em,' I say quickly, and everybody laughs.

Afterwards, I give Angela and Andrea one cigarette each. Angela tells me about Melvin as she smokes it. It's always me she tells, ever since she started going out with him, four weeks ago. It's made her more friends with me, somehow, like in the art-room one morning, one of the first summery kind of mornings, she was all smiles. The two of them were, whispering across the table, with their heads bent low.

'Do... you... know a boy... called Melvin?'

I had shaken my head.

'How come? He's a culluboy... he might be your cousin or something?'

'Dopes!'

But the two of them were smiling so child-like, as if something wonderful and exciting was happening; and it was one of the first summery kinds of days, so that I had to smile too.

Now I listen to Angela while I stack my coins into little piles. They want four kids, two boys and two girls. The little girls will be called 'Jade' and 'Amber'. Andrea pulls a face and so do I, and Angela gets upset when she sees us starting to laugh. 'Orr!' she says. 'Doan you like those names? Doan you? I think they're *gorgeous*, for little girls I do...' She shoves at our shoulders as we move towards the lines. I forget to ask about the boys' names.

It's nearly July now, and I've started mitching off from school. I can't stand it there. The others moan, but they don't hate, so I'm on my own. Mary the elephant tried to find out what was wrong. She mixes me up with another coloured girl, Carmel, who is two forms ahead of me. 'Now just what *is* the matter with you, Carmel, hmm? You seem to have developed a real chip on your shoulder. Would you like to tell me about it, dear?' I just stared at her until she got nasty and sent me away. Of course, I'd known all along she was putting it on.

If it's a nice day I sit in the park, enjoying the sunshine on my arms and legs. Old posh people sit on benches and look at the flowers lined up, row after row in front of them. These benches are hard. Mothers allow their pestering kids to climb up on the wooden slats, then shout at them when they fall and start to cry. I watch the mothers wheel the crying kids away, speeding along, then slowing down, until the kids forget to cry and start to laugh.

Click. Her face never comes into focus properly. It's like cold water blurring up in your eyes. Enormous. You blink and it's gone. Except that I remember the feel of her fingers, parting through my hair, as if it were an undergrowth. 'Let me see you with this – like that, in the front.' When I turned my head to face her, she changed her mind. 'No, I'll have to try it like this. And keep still!' She always said that: 'Keep still, or I'll leave it like it is.'

The butcher's shop had a tiled white coldness about it, with flashes of silver and tucks of green plastic parsley between the trays. The butcher's wife wraps up the meat in triangles of kitchen paper, quickly, before the blood seeps through. After she's given me the change, she reaches over the counter to touch my hair with cold, reddened fingers, 'Look Bill,' she says, 'lambs' tails.'

Sunlight presses on my eyelids like a band and when I open my eyes I have to blink hard before I can see. At four o'clock, I make my way out of the park and walk towards the ornamental gates. When I was about seven or eight I used to tell her everything, stand by the bed and tell her, 'Mama, these two boys said they'd beat me up, Ma, kids are callin' me blackie alla time, nigger, wog, Ma?'

'Tell them you're nine,' she said. 'They'll leave you alone then.'

'But what if they don't?'

She sighed. 'Then tell them — you should say, look, I'm black by nature, I am. Not by dirt, like you lot.'

Yes, I felt better after that, prepared, ready for the next time. Though I couldn't help noticing, when she stood up and walked slowly towards the stairs, that the backs of her legs were white, as white as the packs of lard in the butcher's shop.

I trail my fingers along the park railings, seeing grass and flower beds in vertical strips. Nature clipped and dull. Then I think, 'What is *my* nature?' And all I can see inside my head is a garden of tangled chlorophyll green. Outside the park gates there are men waiting in cars. I remember the first time one of them leaned across the steering wheel and told me to get in. All I did was stare at him. And he stared back as if it was nothing, like opening the door to the rent man, or the insurance man. Now if one of them said anything, I'd just tell him to eff off. And I'd say it over my shoulder as I crossed the road. 'Eff off, y' b— !' But I always wonder, why do they think I'd get in the car with them? Do I look as if I'd jump into a car? With them? I'd never tell him at home, he'd make too much fuss.

Walking up the garden path, I notice that some of the potato plants have started to flower, pretty star-shaped flowers of pale yellow. I lash out with my foot as I go past.

My father is talking about me to Mr Talbot in the front room. I hold the tin-opener in my hand and try to listen. I can't catch what he says exactly, but it's something about me singing. It's true I've taken to singing around the house for some reason, but I don't want Mr Talbot and all of them to know that. Mr Talbot is big and fat. I twist the metal butterfly on the side of the tin-opener. I think of Mr Talbot as a twister, twisting things, twisting out of things, big as he is. Mr Talbot makes it his business to stand on the porch and inspect the potatoes at the end of every visit. Saying how they're coming along nicely, all the while nodding and smiling as if he can't get over it. His own front garden has a lawn and a rockery with a gnome on the top.

'Kids!' I hear him say, and he gives a little laugh. I picture him mopping his head with a large white handkerchief. 'All them gotta mind for is this pop, pop, pop. My Milton is the same — you know but, teacher to tell me that boy coulda gone to a university, I mean to say, Ox-ford, you know? Cam-bridge... but.' There is a small silence until my father mentions the horses. 'You have any luck lately? Me neither, notta shit...'

I remember back to when my father and Mr Talbot were big men, home from sea. And my father would pour out two tots of rum and the both of them would sit and talk, seriously. They would ignore the cakes and biscuits placed in front of them. Men don't eat sweet things, when they're with other men, I think to myself and marvel, as I scoop the tuna fish into a dish.

When I bring the tray into the room, Mr Talbot breaks off in the middle of his speech. He smiles as he takes his cup and saucer. 'So, when she is ready, she will give us a song, eh?' He smiles at my father on the other side of the room, then he looks at me. My face is empty. 'She shy?' he asks my father, and throws back his head to laugh. 'Shy!' His mouth opens up like an archway.

It's August now, and the front garden is empty, cleared. The potatoes have all been dug up and stored in a sack. He was pleased at the amount and the size of them, four or five to a root. I had to stand there and hold the sack. 'Next year,' he said excitedly, 'if God spares you — ' Well, as soon as he said that, I stopped listening and began to clean the dirt from my fingernails.

My arms have been blackened by the sun, but only up to the elbows, like a pair of long evening gloves. In idle moments like these, I picture myself gliding across a stage grandly, microphone in hand, my hair palmed down with coconut oil... but how you supposed to look? I spent the cigarette money on some make-up and a ruched top. The top had gold threads running through it, a basket weave of golden threads that shone when they caught the light. Angela went with me to the boutique. She helped me put the make-up on, then she stood back and put her hands to her mouth. 'Oh my god, Marcia,' she said. 'You looks white, with the make-up on, you do!'

'Orr! piss off,' I said, laughing and scrubbing at my face with a tissue. 'I doan wanna look like none of you lot.' Angela laughed as she tried to stop me wiping it off. 'Now doan be silly,' she said trying to stop my hand. 'Doan be silly now, Marcie... of course you do, of course you do...'

When I tried the top on properly at home, I didn't like the feel of it, dry and scaly like snakeskin. Then I started to pick at the gold threads until I'd unravelled half of it. Rice threads, it was made of rice threads. So cheap the gold flaked off and stuck to the palms of my hands; and I kept looking down at them expecting to see a green tinge, like when you're a kid and you hold a penny in your hand too long.

After the garden was cleared, I tried raking it over, but it didn't look the same as when Mr Blueser did it. The soil is too dry and pebbly now. When I think of Mr Blueser, I always imagine him as a travelling country blues man. Though I've heard my father say that 'Blueser' is really spelt '*Blusa*'. Because that's what he bought, on a trip to South America once, a woman's blouse. My father and Mr Talbot still laugh about how he used to wear it all the time, proud as a peacock, until they forced him to see what it was. 'Chow man for shame! Get rid on dem bloody girl ting.' Mr Talbot says now, that the government will never increase poor Mr Blueser's pension. It will stay at the same rate, always. Three pounds seventeen shillings and sixpence. 'Doan matter how much contribution he pay in over the years. *Tacoma Star* torpedo off in the war an' alla them things is no dem use...'

This summer my body looks as if it's been mapped out in different shades: black; gold; brown. And my hair, after it's been washed, springs up from my head like a rain-forest. An Amazon rain-forest. It seems funny to be thinking about a continent, when you've always been brought up on an island...

STRIPE BY STRIPE

At around about half-past five, two black boys crossed over the back-yard of the maisonettes and headed towards the pub. It had been a very hot day, the sky was still a hazy blue, but the boys were dressed for evening, in black jackets and trousers, frilled white shirts and black bow-ties. From the veranda, Mrs Offiah watched them go. Like a double act, the boys ducked their marcelled heads beneath the empty washing lines, once, twice, three times, then straightening up together they leapt, high over the trampled-down part of the wire netting, and disappeared around the side of the 'Blue Bayou'.

From the second floor veranda Mrs Offiah watched them go. Then she leaned back on her kitchen chair and shouted into the open doorway behind her. 'Arlene! Arlene! Tell that Dalton he's gunna to be late, the other two've gone in.'

Arlene was Mrs Offiah's youngest daughter, and she was thirty-six. Dalton her baby grandson was seventeen.

'Mama, doan shout!' said Arlene from the kitchen now. 'There's plenty of time — the boy haven't finished eating yet. D'you want him with indigestion?'

'Well them other two've gone in,' Mrs Offiah said again, and shifted on her chair.

It was very hot.

A shadow passed across her line of vision as Jock from next door got up from the stool he was sitting on, and came and stood in front of the veranda railings.

'Oh, hello Jock.' Mrs Offiah shaded a hand over her eyes. 'I didn't realise you was still there,' she said. 'You've been so quiet.'

'Aye.' Jock swayed on his feet.

'You going over the pub tonight?'

'Aye.' Jock laid his arms on top of the railings to steady himself. 'I might go on over after,' he said. 'Just to have a look.'

'They've had it all done out — the bar,' said Mrs Offiah. 'American style — beautiful.'

Jock hiccuped. 'American this, American that,' he said. 'Humerican shit don't stink, *hic*. Do it.'

'Heyay now!' Shading her eyes, Mrs Offiah looked towards the stair-well at the far end. 'Yers Miriam coming,' she said. 'Miriam!' she shouted down the length of the veranda, laughing. 'Come and sort him out, will you? He've started.'

'Have you started?'

Miriam lowered two bags of shopping to the concrete floor and drew in her breath. 'You'd better not be starting,' she said. 'I've had enough to put up with, up in town. What a performance!' She turned to Mrs Offiah. 'In the end I had to take a taxi, just to get away from her mouth.'

'Whose mouth?' said Mrs Offiah, 'Whose mouth you talkin' about?'

'Hers down there, Madame Patti's.'

'Oh gord!'

Mrs Offiah lifted her eyes up to heaven. Madame Patti was the good time girl, living in the flat downstairs. Rowing and drinking and causing trouble, painting her front door bright yellow while everyone else's was council house blue. 'Oh gord!' Mrs Offiah said again and listened while Miriam told the business.

'Only a little feller he was,' said Miriam. 'And she threw her arms round him. Lovin' him up, I thought she was going to smother him, me, the size on her.'

'Oh, she've gone one helluva size,' said Mrs Offiah, 'to what she used to be, Patti. It's all the drink — but I bet she called him, did she? Called him rotten from his hole to his pole I 'spect, when he told her no?'

'You're jokin' —'

Voice aggrieved, Miriam stooped to pick up her shopping. 'I was only waiting for the lights to change, *I* was. But it was me she called to pieces. Yeah, stands there waving to him, nice as ninepence as he walks away, then turns on me with her foul mouth. I didn't know where to put my face. But you know what it is —'

Miriam dragged her shopping towards her own front door, and then stopped, half-way. 'You know what it is,' she said looking back over her shoulder with a laugh. 'I'd seen too much, hadn't I? Seen her shown up stupid by one little runt of a thing —' Miriam shifted the bags in her hands and looked at Jock. 'You gunna help me in with this shopping or stand there and watch me strangle myself?'

After the door had closed on them, Mrs Offiah sat for a moment nodding in silence. Then she leaned back on her chair and shouted into the kitchen one last time: 'Dal-ton, Arlene?'

The three of them were outside on the veranda when Madame Patti came back from town.

She wasn't in the best of moods, Madame Patti, what with the heat and everything. It was boiling hot. And what she had on was sticking to her body. Boiling it up. She cursed the little red leather mini skirt she'd forced over her hips that morning; and the matching red leather bomber jacket. The jacket was too tight around the arms — like a goddamn whatchumacallit, she thought, around the arms. My friggin arms'll drop off inna minute.

Tired, she pushed the red leather beatle cap further down on her golden Jerri curls; then she threw her head back to the sky and yawned. It was a big yawn and right in the middle of it she noticed — up there on the veranda, three figures looking down on her.

Well love my frickin neighbours, Madame Patti thought, bemused. If it's not *this* one, it's *that* one down yer — doggin' on me. Alla time doggin'. You goes up town for a birra peace an they're behind you. You comes on home to put your feet up an they're out yer — nosin'. It's no wonder I can't get no luck around yer with that lot, she thought tearfully; then angrily: bastards! Puttin' their bad eye on me...

Upstairs on the veranda they heard her language increase in volume as she tried to turn the key in her front door lock. When the door swung open, she drew her head back and shouted up through the railings in an embittered tone of voice: 'People? Huh, people doan keep me, I keeps myself. But I just wished to Christ these *people* would stop doggin' on me. Thass all.' Then she went inside and slammed the door shut.

'Who she throwing her skits at now?' said Mrs Offiah, hobbling over to the railings and looking down.

'Oh Mama leave it,' said Arlene, kneeling to brush the back of Dalton's suit. 'You waits 'til the woman's gone in —'

'Yeah, Nana, leave it,' said Dalton sternly. 'Keep the peace why doan you, uh?'

The old lady smiled at her baby grandson and hobbled back to her chair. 'Well she doan frighten me,' she said. 'That reprobate.'

Three coaches drew up outside the pub and Dalton pulled at his cuff-links. 'Right then,' he said. 'I'm off.' 'You mind yourself now!' Mrs Offiah was shouting down the veranda after him. 'An if anybody starts, just tell 'em they'll have me to reckon with — your grandmother. Tell 'em that!'

'*La'ys 'n gen'lemen, la'ys 'n gen'lemen*' — *a voice boomed over the speakers at nine o'clock. 'I'm talkin 'bout the good ole days, those good old hey-days, down the Bay days — when this one square mile, that we are all privileged to be in — was like, the New Orleans of a great coaling Metropolis. The days when people thought they'd reached the end of the rainbow, when they reached this spot. This little spot that we calls simply: The Bay. A place where people have fought hard and played hard. Especially, la'ys an' gen'lemen, especially on a Friday Night. Because Friday Night, Was Always Dynamite! down here — in The Bay. An lemme tell you something people — things haven't changed, all that much!*'

'He good ain' he, that Oscar?' Mrs Offiah was listening from the veranda. 'He knows how to talk the place up, my god!'

'That's what you've got to do these days,' said Arlene. 'F you wants to get anywhere — shake your butt and sell your stuff. He told me that 'smornin', when we were cleaning out the bar. He said: "Arlene, we're sitting on a disused gold-mine down yer. With all this new development —"'

Mrs Offiah laughed. 'Oh, he've discovered his roots, he have Oscar. 'Specially now there's money growin' on the end of 'em.'

'If he didn't do it, somebody else would —' Arlene craned her neck over the veranda railings. The lounge in the 'Blue Bayou' was full of smoke and noise and above the thud of the music she could hear the sound of glasses being clinked, and people laughing and joking. Some of them had wandered outside and were dancing the conga on the grass where the old canal used to be. Up and down and around — they seemed to be enjoying themselves at any rate. 'Thinks they're in another country when they comes down yer,' said Arlene, 'the way they lets their hair down, half of 'em.'

'Am I missin' anything?' said Miriam, when she came out on the veranda an hour later.

'Only the hokey-cokey,' said Mrs Offiah. 'They've got that startin' up in a minute.'

'Karaoke!' said Arlene. 'How many times!'

It was a beautiful balmy evening, and the women stayed out on the veranda to enjoy it.

They laughed when they heard Oscar singing '*Strangers In The Night*' over the microphone. He really sounded like him — Frank Sinatra, even though he looked more like Sammy Davies Jnr what with the nose and the chin and everything. 'Hey up,' said Mrs Offiah. 'Ole blue eyes is black, look.'

'You're a racist to your own colour you are,' said Arlene.

'No I'm not,' said Mrs Offiah. 'How am I? Mind,' she turned to Miriam. 'He've had it done out lovely over there, everything brand new. Makes it easier for us cleanin'. He couldn't get over it, how quick we were the 'smornin'. Those two, he tole the brewery man, are like a pair of Russians. The amount of work they gets through — alla muck and vomit – '

'Eurf!' said Miriam, who worked in the pot-pourri factory and always kept her hands nice. 'I couldn't do it I'm sorry — cleanin' up after other people, I couldn't —'

'Well someone's got to do it,' said Arlene. 'It's a case you've got to an' that's that.'

Miriam laughed and tried to change the subject — 'Oh aye,' she said. 'I'm not sayin' —'

But Arlene wasn't finished. 'My boy's down there now, she said, 'workin' as a bouncer — an' you knows yourself he's not one to go lookin' for no trouble —'

'Your boy's workin' as a bouncer?' Miriam rose on tippy toes to have a look. 'Oh my gosh.' She recognised the gangling figure standing in front of the entrance, hands behind his back, legs spaced apart. 'He's gone and had his hair cut,' she said, 'right down to the wood!'

'Oh yes, he's in the army now,' said Mrs Offiah. 'The army of the night, he is.'

Almost on cue, Dalton turned his head and looked towards the veranda. 'Whoo-ooh!' the women called and waved to him. 'Whoo-ooh!'

They saw him frown and pull his shoulders back. Then he jabbed his index finger at the doorway behind his mother. *Go on inside* he mouthed the words silently — *Now!*

'Who's he giving his orders to?' Arlene was leaning over the railings in a flash: 'Who you giving your orders to? I'm your mother I am. That's right!' she called out after him. 'That's right, goan find yourself a woman, son, you're not my husband yet!'

She came back to her chair, laughing. 'He's gone,' she said. 'I've shown him up. He's gone round the other side to get away from me.'

Down in the pub, someone dragged Jock to the microphone. Upstairs on the veranda, they heard his drunken voice gargling through a Satchmo song: Bloop doopy doop/ bloop doopy doop/ Bloop doopy doop/ doop doop doop doop/ Oh! what did I do / To be so/ black and blue!

It was only the chorus, and Jock always sang it when he was

109

three sheets to the wind. There was stamping and cheering when he got to the end. 'Used to sing the *whoole* thing once,' he said to Oscar, who was helping him back to his seat. 'Before the niffen coal-dust got to me. I was down the mines I was mun, for thirty-odd years I was.' Jock thumped his chest experimentally and coughed.

'I'll swing for him,' Miriam was saying up on the veranda. 'I will, I'll swing for him.' Arlene and her mother smiled sympathetically, they knew she was only saying that for something to say.

Then Miriam saw Madame Patti coming out of the pub, arm in arm with a stubby looking man that no-one knew. The man had a white blond beard that bristled on his chin, like a nylon scrubbing brush. The two of them were laughing and falling all over the place. The man kept shaking his head and shouting, 'Nine! Nine!'

'Someone ought to report her,' said Miriam. 'For keeping a shanty-house because that's what she's doin' —'

'Not very nice, is it?' said Mrs Offiah, standing up to get a better look. 'Her father must be turning in his grave the poor ole feller because he was a proud old African — fought for the British in Mesopotamia and all you know. Along with your own father, god rest his soul.' She crossed herself and looked at Arlene.

'Oh, Mama! Don't start talkin' about all that again,' said Arlene. 'All that Lloyd George business, and how he did the dirty on all the coloureds in 1919 — people doan wanna h'year about all that again. Jeez,' she laughed and leaned forward. 'Any case I blames Social, I do. For Madame Patti. They were the ones who wouldn't give the girl the money to buy new stuff when her cooker broke down and everything. Only a loan they told her. Only a loan that's all we're allowed to give you. She told me herself, "Arlene," she said "this Gover'ment wants see me 'self-supportin' so I am. I am self-supportin'. I've bought a new bed," she said, "an' it's king-size!"'

'What!' Miriam's voice rose to the bait and she was about to

110

start ranting and raving when a terrific 'bang' went off outside the pub. In the sudden silence, they heard the tinkling sound of falling glass. Then the thud of footsteps running. Then nothing, not a whisper as everything went quiet and Mrs Offiah began to scream: 'It's a bomb! It's a bomb! It's a bomb gone off—'

Even as she was screaming a police-van drew up outside the pub and six policemen opened the van doors and jumped out, two at a time, as if by magic. It didn't seem real. Miriam and Arlene knocked over their chairs and ran, down the stairs and across the yard, both of them holding their hands to their terrified throats.

'Me, I flew,' said Arlene. She turned her face up to the morning sky and laughed, awestruck at the memory of her own panic. 'I said you're not having him! What are you taking him for? Why doan you arrest the ones that caused the trouble; not him!'

She looked across at Dalton and laughed. They were all sat outside on the veranda, taking in the fresh air and resting, after the upsets of the night before. Dalton leaned his chin on the back of the chair he was straddling. Smiling he raised one arm like a boxer, acknowledging the crowd's applause. Then he reached down and grabbed an imaginary bottle of wine from the floor. Smiting the air in front of him, he shouted: 'Pow! They couldn't touch me, right? Pow! they couldn't touch me. Oscar shouts: "there's money missin' from the till. There's money missin'!" So I picks up this bottle of Bacardi, calm as could be, runs after 'em. These four guys right. I runs after 'em, an — Pow! I puts the Bacardi through their windscreen. Stops 'em drivin' off. End of story.'

'End of story, end of story!' said Arlene. 'They would've had you up for causing criminal damage if it hadn't been for me. Lemme see that bump they gave you, look at the swellin'! — I told 'em — it's a pity you don't stick with what you're supposed to be doing. Instead of dragging off the innocent. Come their nonsense, I said: yer, an' I held out my hands. Yer I said h'you

111

are: I'm his mother, put the handcuffs on me, I'm responsible for his colour.' She laughed. 'What! they're too much of it the police. Sees everything in black and white, I told 'em.' She laughed. 'Think they were glad to see the back of me! Time I finished —'

'No Mama,' Dalton's voice was patient as he weaved from side to side, feinting jabs and uppercuts. 'Pow!' He turned to her. 'Oscar would've sorted everything out for me; no sweat. He's the boss —'

'Oscar sets the balls for other people to fire,' said Miriam quietly. They waited for her to say something else, but she didn't elaborate. She looked tired, standing in the doorway with her arms folded, keeping an eye on Jock. Jock sat on a stool in front of her, boozed. Every so often he'd slide forward, and she'd reach out her arm and drag him back, shouting into his face: 'You'll fall if you don't keep still! D'you wanna fall on your face a second time, uh?'

Jock's face was dirty. And there was a deep cut on his cheekbone where he'd fallen over. Or been pushed over more like, thought Miriam. Remembering how the people had crowded out of the pub doors and into the night. The high point of their evening's entertainment, she thought. Remembering the faces, tickled pink, the faces — watching and laughing as the police tried to arrest the bouncer along with the thieves — while Jock lay on the floor rolling drunk and yodelling at the top of his voice. Blood all over the place, like rum and black on the pavement. It was mortifying. Being on show for people, those type of people. Jock had lost his shirt somewhere along the line, and he was sitting in his vest and trousers.

'Look at you,' Miriam shouted suddenly. 'Anybody'd think you'd just got back from doing a hard day's work, to look at you.'

Jock's head jerked backwards. His mouth fell open and he smiled up at her, half stupid with drink. Then his head went forward again, and he started droning into his chest, like Louis Armstrong: 'Oh, what did I do / to be so black 'n blue?'

112

For some reason Miriam felt like crying. Just laying her head down somewhere she thought; and bursting out crying. She was glad when Arlene stood in front of her with a hot cup of tea. 'I've had a sickener of it, I have,' she said, accepting the steaming cup. 'A bloody sickener. Pardon my language.'

Then they heard a voice shouting up from the yard. 'I'm putting you all on a warnin'! Are you listening up there?' It was Madame Patti, standing in the middle of the yard with a paint brush and a five litre can of yellow paint in her hands. 'Parking lines I've got down yer now,' she yelled. 'Nosey bleedin' parking lines! Double yellow, are you listening?' No-one up on the veranda said anything.

Jock took a sip of his tea and then stopped, as if he'd done something wrong. 'Whose round is this?' he kept saying, trying to get up from his seat. 'Whose round is it?'

'Just shurrup an' drink it!' said Miriam, pushing him back on the stool.

'Yeah, drink it,' said Mrs Offiah. 'It's on the house,' she said, 'it's on the house,' and everyone laughed into their teacups and they finished their tea.

MAMA'S BABY
(PAPA'S MAYBE)

Two summers ago, just after I'd turned fifteen, my mother got ill. One night in our flat on the twelfth floor, she held her face in both hands and said, 'Leisha, I'm sure I got cancer!'

'Just so long as you haven't got AIDS,' I said, and carried on munching my tacos and watching the telly. The tacos were chilli beef'n jalapeño. Hot. Very hot. With a glistening oily red sauce that ran down my chin as I spoke.

'AIDS?' I remember her voice sounded bewildered. 'What're you talking about, AIDS? How the hell could I have AIDS?' She grabbed at my shoulder. 'I'm an agoraphobic, I don't hardly go out...'

I took my eyes away from the television set and stared at her face. Then I just busted out laughing. I couldn't help myself. I was almost choking. Loretta looked at me as if she didn't know me. As if I belonged to somebody else. 'J-O-K-E,' I said, catching my breath and wiping my chin. 'Laugh, Muvver!' But she couldn't do that, laugh. Even when I spelt it out for her. 'Like, AIDS'n agoraphobia – they're mutually exclusive, right? So you haven't got it Lol, have you?' She still didn't laugh. She couldn't laugh or be brave or anything like that, my mother Loretta.

All she could do was hit me with a slipper and call me stupid. 'Orr, Mama!' I rubbed at my arm, pretending to be hurt. 'You can't take a joke, you can't.'

'No, it's no jokin' with you.' Loretta got angry as she looked at me. 'You're gunna bring bad luck on people you are,' she said. 'With your laughin' an jokin'!'

Bring bad luck by laughing? Such stupidness, I thought, in my own mother. Then I noticed how her body kept shivering as she sat there, squashed into the corner of our plush red settee. And how she couldn't keep her hands still, even though they were clamped together tight. So tight, that the knuckle bones shone through. 'Cancer's a bad thing, Aleisha.' My mother shook her head from side to side, and started to cry. 'A bad thing!'

'Orr Mama, you talks rubbish, you do.' She looked at me through streaming eyes. 'How do I?' she said. 'How do I talk rubbish?'

I shrugged. 'You just do.'

I remembered what she'd said about tampons. Loretta said tampons travelled twice round the body at night, then lodged in your brain. Fact. Even the nuns in school laughed at that one. They said what my mother told me was unproven, unscientific and an old wives' tale. Stupidness!

Now Loretta was sitting there, crying and talking about cancer. I wished she'd stop. The crying made her dark eyes shine like windows, when the rain falls on them at night. There was light there, but you couldn't see in. Not really. It was like staring into the blackness of outer space. And it made me mad.

'Look, why don't you just stop crying,' I said, adopting a stern voice, a mother's voice. A sensible voice. 'And get to the doctor's first thing tomorrow morning and see about yourself?'

Loretta looked at me and hiccuped. Then she started crying again. Louder than before. 'Just phone Joe,' she said through her sobs. 'Phone that boy for me, Leish. I want that boy with me.'

'Okey-dokey.' I took another big mouthful of taco and chewed callously. It was out of my hands now. Now Loretta had asked for Joe. Let Joe deal with it. I stood up. 'Where's your twenty pence pieces then?'

I went off to the call box with the taste of Mexican takeaway still in my mouth. Joe was out with the boys, so I left a message with Donna, who was full of concern. 'Is it serious?' she said.

'Nah.' I burped silently into the night as the tacos came back

115

to haunt me. 'It's not serious,' I said. 'But you know Loretta.' My nostrils burned and my eyes filled up with water. 'You knows my mother, once she gets an idea into her head...'

Donna laughed brightly and said not to worry. She'd tell Joe as soon as he came in. 'Yeah, tell him,' I said. Raising my voice as the time ran out and the pips began to bleep. 'Though it's probably nothing. Something an' nothing. Knowin' her.'

I was wrong of course. I was wrong about everything under the sun and under the moon. But what did I know? I was fifteen years old that summer, and mostly, I thought like a child.

Like when I was six, nearly seven, I found a big blue ball hidden in the cupboard of the wall unit. I brought the ball out and placed it on the floor. Then I tried to step up and stand on it. I fell off, but I kept on trying. Again and again and again. All I wanted to do was to stand on the big blue ball that had misty swirls of white around it. Like the swirls I'd seen on satellite pictures of planet earth.

When I finally managed it – arms outstretched and my feet successfully planted, I felt like a conqueror. A six-year-old conqueror. 'Orr look at this!' I yelled at Joe. 'Look Joe, look!' I stayed upright for another dazzling moment. Then the ball rolled under me and I fell backwards, screaming as my head hit the floor. Loretta came out of the bathroom with a face pack on. She silenced me with a slap. Then she took the comic Joe was reading and threw it in the bin. 'Naw, Ma,' said Joe. 'That's my *Desperate Dan* that is.'

'Too bad,' said Loretta. 'Maybe it'll teach you to look after this kid when I tell you!'

Joe laid his head down on the pine-top table, sulking, while I sat on the edge of our scrubby, rust-red carpet and hugged my knees. I wasn't worried about Joe getting into trouble on account of me. All I was worried about was the ball. The beautiful blue ball. More than anything in the world I wanted it back.

But Loretta had snatched the ball away from me and was holding it up to the light. Palming it over and over in her hands.

As if she was searching for something. But what? What magical thing could she be searching for? I watched the ball turn blue under the light bulb. Then not so blue, then *bluer* again. And it came to me in flash – that what my mother was doing was remembering.

But remembering what? Her creamy face was cracking into brown, spidery lines as she looked at the ball. And I got up on my knees, wanting to see more.

'*Bug-eyes!*' Joe leaned down from the corner of the table and hissed at me. 'Fathead,' he said. 'You boogalooga bug-eyed fathead!' Joe's words put a picture inside my head that made me cry. I opened my mouth and bawled until Loretta turned round. Her face had stopped cracking, and she looked ordinary. 'Joe!' she said, 'how old are you for god's sake? Tormentin' that kid. She's younger than you.'

'She's a *alien*,' said Joe.

'Oh don't be so bloody simple!' Loretta looked across the room at me. 'She's your sister.' Joe shook his head. 'She's *not* my sister.' He kicked at the leg of the table with his big brown chukka boot. 'She's my *half*-sister,' he said.

I remember the words were hardly out of Joe's mouth before Loretta had reached him. 'Half?' she said. 'Half?' She started bouncing the big blue ball upside his head. 'Who taught you half? I didn't give birth to no halves!'

Loretta was mad at Joe. So mad she kept banging the ball against his head. As if she was determined to knock some sense in. Until Joe (who was twelve, and big for his age) lifted his big chubby arms in front of his face and yelled at her. 'Get off've me! Fuckin' get off've me. Right!'

I was scared then. I thought Joe was in for a hiding. The mother and father of a hiding. But something strange happened, Loretta suddenly upped and threw the ball away from her – just threw it, as if she was the one who was hurt. And as soon as she let the ball go, wonder of wonders, Joe burst into tears and pushed his head against her belly. Sobbing out loud like a baby, saying, 'It's not fair! It's not fair!' And asking her over and over again as she cwtched him, 'How come *my* father never brought *me* no presents, Ma? How come?'

Poor Joe! I sat in the middle of our scrubby red carpet happily hugging the big blue ball to myself. I realised now that I was luckier than Joe. My *half*-brother Joe. And quicker than Joe and cleverer than Joe – even though I looked like a *alien*. Joe was like Loretta. I looked across the room at them, across the scrubby, rust-red carpet, which suddenly stretched out vast and empty as the red planet Mars.

'You takes after *my* family,' Loretta was telling Joe. 'You takes after *me*.' I felt a pang, but it didn't matter. I had the blue ball – which was big enough to stand on, like planet earth. A special ball, bought for me specially, by a strange and wonderful person called *my dad*!

Of course, *my dad* was always more of an idea than anything else. I never saw my real dad when I was a kid. But I clung to the idea of him. In the same way that I clung to an image of myself at six, triumphantly balancing on a blue, rolling ball. They were secret reminders of who I really was. I held on to those reminders even more when Loretta was diagnosed as having cancer. They helped me keep my distance. And I needed to keep my distance, because once the hospital people dropped the big C on her for definite – cancer of the womb (Intermediary Stage) things got scary. And while Joe tried to pretend that nothing terrible was happening, or would happen, I knew better. And I made sure I kept my distance from the start.

Like when Loretta had to travel back and forth to the Cancer Clinic for treatment. Joe asked if I'd go with her. 'Sometimes,' he said, 'just to keep her company?'

'I can't,' I said. 'I've got tests coming up in school.'

'Tests?' Joe looked at me gone off. 'Tha' Mama's sick,' he said. 'She needs someone with her. I can't go myself cuz I'm in work.' His jaw tightened.

118

'I've got a biology test coming up, I said. And maths and history...'

'Oh leave it Joe,' said Loretta. 'I'm all right!' She laughed, 'I'll manage.' Joe umm'd and ah'd a bit, then he gave in.

'If you're sure, Ma,' he said. Hiding a little smile, I picked up my biology textbook, *The Language of the Genes*, and began taking seriously detailed notes.

I never did go with Loretta to the Cancer Clinic. Though I could have made time, if I'd wanted. Academic work was easy for me, I enjoyed reading books and doing essays. And tests were almost a doddle. But at home I began making a big thing of it. Hiding behind the high wall of 'my schoolwork' and 'my classes' and my sacrosanct GCSEs, which I wasn't due to sit until the following year anyway.

I also let it be known that I had to go out, nights. Most nights, otherwise I'd turn into a complete mental brainiac.

So when Loretta arrived home weak and vomiting from the radium treatment, I'd already be standing in front of the mirror, tonging my hair, or putting on eye make-up. No need to ask where I was going. I was off out, to enjoy myself. Even though enjoying myself meant drinking (alcopops) and smoking, and hanging with the crowd. All the stuff I used to describe as 'too boring and predictable' for anyone with half a brain. Now though, it was different. Now I became best mates with a hard-faced, loud-mouthed girl called Cookie, who Loretta said was 'wild'.

The euphemism made me smile as I rushed around the kitchen filling the kettle and making the tea to go in the flask. I was happy and focused on what I had to do, knowing that the sooner Loretta was settled, the sooner I'd be out through the door.

Luckily, there was no need to bother with food. Loretta couldn't swallow any food. Only Complan. And Complan made her vomit. So she stuck to tea. Weak tea, and sometimes, a couple of mouthfuls of tinned soup. Which I did think was sad, because my mother was a big woman who'd always enjoyed her food.

Now, she hardly ever went in the kitchen, and it wasn't worth bothering to try and tempt her with anything. But I brought her a cup of tea, and handed it over. And I put the flask on the little table next to the couch.

Taking a couple of sips of tea seemed to exhaust her. And she laid her head back on the cushions, tired, but not too tired to speak. 'This girl Cookie...' she said.

'Yeah?' By now I'd gone back to the mirror and my mascara.

'I don't like the idea of you runnin' round with her.' Loretta pursed her lips. 'That girl's trouble,' she said. 'That girl's hot!' I was watching Loretta's face in the mirror. Her face and my face, side by side. It was eerie seeing us together. Like watching night turn into day or day turn into night. There was no resemblance between us. No real likeness that I could see. And it played on my mind. Who was she, I thought? This big woman lying on a plush red couch, with a green plaid blanket pulled up to her chin? I crossed over to the couch and looked at her, coldly. 'What're you talking about, hot?' I said. 'You're always going on about something.'

Loretta sighed. 'I just don't want you in no trouble,' she said. 'You nor Joe, come to that.'

'I'm not gunna be in any trouble!'

'No?' Loretta looked up at me and smiled. 'Well, God be good,' she said, 'let's hope it'll stay like that.'

'Listen,' I brought my face down close to hers and spoke slowly, deliberately. 'Cookie's ways, are not my ways, right?' My voice grew colder. 'Your ways, are not my ways...' Loretta stared at my face, as if she couldn't understand what I was saying. Then she took a gulp of tea and her eyes swam with tears.

'You little bitch,' she said. 'Anybody'd think I was a bad mother to h'yer you speak!' The sudden energy in her voice surprised me. And I tried to back away from what I'd started. But Loretta was on a roll. 'Did I get rid of you?' she said. 'Did I? No, I kept you. You and Joe. Even though I had no man behind me. And what's my thanks?' Her voice was angry as she spoke to me. Loud and angry. 'Shit is my thanks!'

I shrugged and tried to move away, but she started off again. "Course, it'd be different if I was posh, wouldn't it?'

'Pardon?' I said.

'They gets rid of their kids in a minute. Don't they, posh women? When they wants to go to *college* or something.' Loretta looked up at the ceiling and laughed. 'An' no bugger ever says a word,' she said, disbelievingly. 'Not a bloody word!'

For some reason I found myself laughing along with her. Enjoying the unfairness of it all. Then she closed her eyes again, tired. 'Look, *get* if you're going,' she said. 'And don't be back yer late.'

When I reached the door, I turned to look at her. 'D'you want this light left on?'

'No, out it.' So I flicked the switch and left her there, in the dark.

It was always a big relief to me when Loretta was taken into hospital.

I was happy then, escorting her down to the waiting ambulance and handing her in. It felt as though we were celebrities, touched by a black and tragic glamour, as the neighbours rushed out of their flats and gave Loretta cards, and waved her off, like royalty.

Back inside, I always walked slowly past the lifts in the entrance hall. Then I'd whizz around the corner and start bounding up the stairs. Two at a time. All the way up to the twelfth floor.

The first few times Loretta went into hospital, I stayed with Joe and Donna in their little two-bedroomed house. But I didn't feel comfortable there. And when Loretta began to spend longer and longer as an inpatient, I told Joe I preferred to stay where I was, and keep an eye on the flat. Joe stuck out his jaw and said, 'If that's what you want, Aleisha. I'm not gunna argue.'

Which was just what I expected him to say. Though I hated him for saying it. After that, it wasn't difficult for me to ease my way out of things, bit by bit.

Whenever I made an appearance at the hospital, I was never

on my own. I always came in with a crowd – usually Cookie and her sister, Cherry. Or Cookie and her new man friend, Wayne. I think they liked being with me, because I was fifteen years old and my mother was dying of cancer. It was like something off the telly that appealed to them.

Joe never came in on his own, either. He was always with Donna or one of his mates – usually Deggsie, or a caramel-coloured boy called Chip-chip, whose teeth were brown and white, like popcorn.

With so many young people around Loretta's bed, there was never any time for seriousness. All we could do was lark and joke about. Once, when they were fooling around, Joe and Chip-chip pressed down on the foot-pedals of the bed. Sending Loretta up in the air. And all she did was laugh and say, 'Put me down, boys! Put me down, people can see my old blue slippers under there.'

It was odd, standing under the bright hospital lights, watching Loretta laughing. And Joe laughing. All of us laughing, as if everything was right with the world. Loretta was queen of the show. She sparkled in company, which was the way she used to be, I suppose, when she was young and working in pubs as a barmaid.

One night, Joe and Donna came in carrying a bouquet of flowers between them.

Loretta didn't care much for the white chrysanthemums, but she was chuffed with the card: '*Happy memories, luv from R. (The Rover).*' R. was Royston, Joe's father. And he'd been on friendly speaking terms ever since Joe had left school, and met up with him again.

'Now he sends me the white bouquet,' said Loretta. 'Maybe he wants to marry me...' While we were laughing, Donna said soppily, 'Why didn't you marry him, Lol?'

'Marry Royston? Prrrrf!' Loretta's voice was derisive. 'He was no good, him, Royston.' She looked at us. 'I put his bags outside the door, didn't I? Comin' his little ways. I said goodbye, tara, I'm sorry – I needs my space!'

'Orr, my poor father! I bet you gave that man a hard time,' said Joe, laughing. I was in agonies in case anyone mentioned *my* father. But luckily the nurse came round, ringing the handbell so we had to go. Good job too, because I would have hated to hear Loretta start in on my dad.

As we were leaving, Joe leant over the bed and asked Loretta in a low voice, about her blood count. When she told him it was up a couple of points, Joe looked relieved. 'Good work Ma,' he said. And went off happily with Donna.

Joe never asked the doctors anything. He clung to his ignorance like a baby clinging to a bottle, and I despised him for it.

My own behaviour was more rational. Gradually, I dropped off going to the hospital on a regular basis. Telling everyone I was studying hard for my 'mocks'. Where we lived, no one understood about 'mocks' and when they were due. Instead, relatives and friends of my mother admired my determination in carrying on with my schooling. You keep it up girl, they said. You're makin' your mother proud!

No one, not even Joe seemed to realise what I was up to. Though I saw my mother less and less, I always made sure I phoned the hospital regularly. 'How is she?' I'd ask dutifully. And I'd end by saying, 'Please give her my love.'

But instead of studying, I spent my time lying on the old red couch where Loretta used to lay, dreaming about my life in the future. 'My dad' was somewhere out there, in the future. I knew his name (from my birth certificate) and that he'd cared enough about me to leave me a gift – the beautiful blue ball. These days, the blue ball looked like a sunken moon, stuck on top of the wall unit. But I treasured its memory, knowing that one day in the starry future, I'd meet my dad, and we'd talk about this gift he'd given me. Of course, we'd recognise each other instantly – my dad and I, because it was obvious to me, that his genes were the dominant genes in my make-up. They were there, encoded in the double helix of my DNA. How else could I account for me?

It was strange how pleasantly the time passed when I was

thinking like this. Even when I did put in an appearance at school, I didn't let go of the daydreams. And when scary night times came around, I'd turn up the mattress on Loretta's bed, and fish out some notes. Then I'd go off with Cookie and the gang, drinking.

Not that I did much drinking, except for a couple of cans of *Hooch*. Three cans of *Hooch* and I was away. Floating. Doing stupid things. Once, I tried to walk around the side of a mirror in the pub toilets. I couldn't see that the toilet door was a reflection – and I kept banging my head on the faecal-coloured wall tiles, as I tried to go round it. The side of my head was swollen and smarting when I stopped.

'Leisha man you makes me piss!' said Cookie, laughing. 'You really do!' It crossed my mind to ask her why I was so funny. And why was she Cookie, and her sister Cherry, so cool? Both of them wore shiny auburn wigs, like supermodels. And they had the clothes. But Cherry was humungous in size. And Cookie wasn't much smaller. So how come they were cool?

I opened my mouth to ask – but I couldn't fit the words inside the moment. The moment just went by me. Pass. So I opened my mouth a bit wider, and started to laugh.

Coming home from a night out, I'd crash down on the old red couch and fall asleep, happy and floating. But in the morning, even before I was awake, I'd feel the weight of something miserable pressing down on me. My eyes would focus slowly, and I'd remember what it was.

Then one day, I woke up and saw a piece of blue sky through the window. I realised it was spring, and for some reason, that made me feel better. So I went and phoned Joe's house, to check up on hospital visiting times; and to see who was going in that night.

The minute she picked up the phone and heard my voice, Donna broke down in tears. 'Wassamarrer?' I said, suddenly fearful. There was a long snuffly silence. Then Donna managed to tell me what had happened. She said the consultant had called Joe up to the hospital and explained there was nothing more they could do. Treatment-wise, that was it. 'Oh, Leisha! I'm so sorry,' said Donna sobbing all over again. 'But there's no hope for her. There's no hope for Loretta!'

It sounded like the title of a book, the way she said it: '*No Hope for Loretta*.' That was my first thought. Then I began to feel empty, as though a stone had dropped inside me. And I needed to sit down, but I couldn't because I was in a call box.

'How're we gunna tell her?' I said, helplessly.

'Oh don't you do anything,' said Donna, quickly. 'Leave it to Joe, Leish. Joe said he'll deal with it.' So feeling especially childish and helpless, I rang off.

I didn't do any of the things I might have done, like phone the hospital. Or actually go in and see my mother. Instead, on a sudden whim, I lifted the telephone book out of the cubbyhole and began flicking through its pages, idly at first, then with more attention. It was gone ten when I arrived in school. Calmly, I sat through classes until lunchtime. Then I picked up my bag and my jacket, and left.

Once out of the school gates I turned right, and onto the high road that ran past the school. I walked slowly, admiring the big solid houses, with their spacious lawns and double-garages. In this area where my school was, all the houses had names instead of numbers. And I said them to myself as I walked along: '*Hawthorns, Erw Lon, Primrose View, Ty Cerrig, Sovereign Chase...*' names that were as anonymous as numbers, really. But I didn't mind. It was a lovely day, warm and sunny, and I kept looking up at the blue sky, marvelling at how beautiful a day it was.

When I came to a black and white gabled house, with a big front lawn and a wrought-iron gate marked *Evergreen*, I stopped. This was the place where the man who could be my dad lived. Blyden, D. H. I'd got the name out of the telephone directory that morning. It was almost the same as the one written on my birth certificate under father: 'David H. Blyden, O/S Student.' It could be him, I reasoned. It could be my dad, living here in a mock-

Tudor house with mullioned windows. Loretta had never had much to say about him, except that he was quiet. But he had his little ways, she said, like they all do. Joe had whispered to me once, that my dad was from Africa. But would an African be living around here? Maybe, I thought, if he had money.

The detached house, like all the surrounding houses, was set well back from the road. And on one side there were no neighbours. Only a red-brick observatory and a fenced-in tennis court. It was all in keeping, I decided approvingly. Everything was so quiet, and cultivated and tasteful. Then, afraid someone might be watching from the window, I walked up onto the grassy bank, nearer the observatory, and sat down.

Now I could see the house from the side, facing the sun, with the dark pine tree towering over it. The pine tree was striking. Its dark green branches seemed to flip out like arrows, right up into the blue sky. As though, I thought admiringly, they were aiming straight into the heart of heaven.

I wondered about my dad, living here. I wondered if he visited the observatory at night, to study the billions of stars in the universe? If he did, he'd understand just how little our lives were, compared to the vast infinity of outer space. Surely he would? He was the man who had given me the blue ball.

I don't know how long I sat there, dreaming and wondering in the sun.

I imagined my African dad, climbing the steps of the observatory, and looking out over the mysteriously empty ball court. Like a priest in ancient Mexico – except that we were in Wales. Our history class that morning had been about lost civilisations – which was a theory connecting Africa to ancient America and to ancient, Celtic Britain. *We were all connected*! I suppose that fed into my mind, and kept my thoughts turning over, magically.

It was late in the afternoon when I heard the sound of car wheels crunching over gravel. Someone was parking a car in front of the house. I got to my feet in a sudden panic. What if it was him, my dad, arriving home? My heart began to pound, and I felt sick. This could be him, I thought with wonder. This could be my dad! Involuntarily, I looked towards the house, and my courage began to waver. Could it be my dad, back there? It was possible, I knew it was possible, but was it probable?

No, I decided, suddenly. No! The sun had disappeared behind the clouds, making everything seem different. Devoid of magic, colder. I glanced up at the observatory, and was amazed to see its structure in a new cold light. Now it was revealed as squat and ugly. Shaped like a red-brick kiln against the sky. I looked again, and saw that its narrow windows or apertures were shuttered over with grey metal grilles. There was a padlock on the entrance door; and weeds were sprouting from the brickwork. The place was derelict!

And there was no mysterious ball court. Just an ordinary tennis court marked out with yellow lines, behind the trampled wire netting. Enough was enough. I swung my bag up over my shoulder, and started walking, fast. I didn't look behind me, not even for a last glimpse of *Evergreen*, with its lonesome pine tree standing dark and arrow like against the sky.

Of course, running away like that allowed me to keep on dreaming. And even before I was halfway home, I'd begun to reassemble my defences. After all, nothing had happened. I could always go there again, I reasoned. Not straightaway, but one day. When I was ready. The choice was mine...

By the time I stepped out of the lift on the twelfth floor, I was actually smiling. It was fun trying to picture myself living with my dad, in a big gabled house, a wrought iron gate and a plaque on the front, marked *Evergreen*.

I was still smiling as I put the key in the lock and gave the door a push. When it swung open, I almost collapsed. Loretta was framed in the doorway, wrapped in a red velvet dressing gown, staring at me. 'Ullo stranger,' she said, in a croaky voice. 'Wassamarrer with you, seen a ghost?'

Inside the living room I was surprised to see how everything had been changed round. The old red couch had been pushed to one side and Loretta's bed had been brought in and placed against the wall. I didn't see Joe at first, hunkered down by the little table, fixing a plug on the lamp. When I did see him, I gave a sigh of relief. 'Oh Joe!' I said, 'you're here!' Joe nodded over his shoulder at me, and carried on with what he was doing.

I watched Loretta move slowly across the room. Twice she had to stop and retie the belt on her dressing gown, as it came undone. Then very gingerly and carefully, she lowered herself onto the edge of the bed, and looked at me. I was terrified. 'What're you doing home?' I said, in a rush. 'I didn't know you were coming home...' Loretta began to laugh. 'She wants to know what I'm doing home, Joe,' she said, looking over her shoulder at him. 'Shall we tell her?'

'Uh, Ma?' said Joe. Too busy screwing a light bulb into the lamp it seemed, to pay much attention. But Loretta didn't need his support. Instead, turning back to me with her dark eyes shining, she leaned forward and whispered, 'I'm home because I'm cured! Ain' I Joe?' she sang out loudly. 'Ain' I cured, almost?'

At that moment, Joe clicked the switch on the table lamp. Throwing a soft, glowing light over everything. Including our faces. 'There!' he said, turning round at last. 'Sixty watts so it won't burn.' He grinned. 'That's better, ain' it?'

A week later I ran away from home, and two days after that, my mother died. I suppose there was something inevitable about the way those two events were linked. But it didn't seem like that at the time.

That last week, I played along with Joe and Loretta as far as I could. What did I care? And on the Thursday night, when I'd had enough, I went out clubbing with Cookie and Cherry. It wasn't really clubbing. We ended up sitting in the Community Centre, because I was broke and Cookie announced, suddenly, that she was saving up for a white wedding.

I asked how much it would cost, a white wedding? 'Thousand pounds,' said Cookie, proudly. 'The dress alone'll set me back a couple a hundred.'

'Wow.'

'That's because she wants one that flows,' said Cherry.

'Yeah, that dress just gorra to be fl-o-w-i-n'!, man,' said Cookie, snapping her fingers and laughing.

I was troubled in mind, but I laughed along with them. Just to show willing. I even asked about the car. What sort of car would they be having? And Cookie said, 'One with wheels, preferably!' And while we were laughing at that, a man came over and asked if he could buy me a drink.

When I said no thanks, he walked away. All nice and polite and everything, but Cookie said I was simple.

'He had a fuckin' big gold ring on his finger!'

'Yeah,' said Cherry. 'And that twenny pound note he was flashing came off've a roll!'

'So?'

'So,' said Cookie, 'anybody'd think you won the lottery!'

For some reason, I lost my temper and started shouting. I told Cookie if I won the lottery, I'd buy *her* a friggin' ticket to Mars. 'And Joe,' I said loudly, 'I'd buy Joe a ticket to Mars, straight off!' Just then a hand tapped me on the shoulder, and I froze. Cookie and Cherry burst out laughing. They knew I thought it was Joe. But it wasn't Joe, when I turned round. Only his best mate, Chip-chip, wanting to say hello. Naturally he asked how my mother was, and I said fine. She's fine. Then Cookie and Cherry went off to the toilets, and Chip-chip pulled up a stool and sat down. He told me he was working part-time, now. In McDonald's, Mickey D's? 'But really,' he said, 'I'm a *player*.'

'A player?'

'Didn't Joe ever tell you?' he said. 'I plays basketball.'

'Oh, yeah,' I said, unenthusiastically, 'basketball!'

'Hey, don't say it like that,' said Chip-chip. He pulled a face at the way I said it, making me laugh. '*Barsketbawl*!'

'I didn't say it like that!'

'Yes you did,' said Chip-chip. 'Still, it's good to see you smiling, I like to see you smiling,' he said. And he went off and bought us both a soft drink, to celebrate.

'Well kiss to that!' said Cookie, coming back to the table half an hour later. 'Lemonade and no major money? An' having to listen to all that stuff about sport is fuckin' boring!' she said. I agreed. But I still thought it was nice for him. Having an interest like basketball. 'His little life is rounded by an O,' I said, half seriously. Then I laughed and got up to dance, when the man with the gold ring on his finger came over and asked me.

While I was dancing, someone tapped me on the shoulder. I looked round with a smile on my face, thinking it was Chip-chip.

But it was Joe. I shied away from him. But he raised his arm and brought his fist crashing down on my back, again and again. 'Where's your mother?' he said, as he punched me. 'I'll tell you where,' he said, punching me. 'She's in the hospital dying,' he said, punching me. 'And where are you? Out!' he said, punching me. 'Enjoyin' yourself!'

Joe only allowed Donna to grab hold of his arm when he'd finished. Then the two of them walked out of the Centre, arm in arm.

Most of the sympathy was on my side. People said Joe was taking everything out on me when I wasn't to blame. Neither of us was to blame, they said; and I knew it was true.

But still, I felt guilty. Before going out that night, I'd brought Loretta her cup of tea and her tablets, and watched her swallow them. Eyeing my outfit, she'd asked if I was going out? 'Yes, I'm going out,' I said, coldly. 'I can go out, can't I? *Now you're on the road to recovery...*'

Loretta didn't say anything after that. And I waited until the tablets knocked her out 'dead' as she always said, then I put on my coat and switched off the light; and left her. An hour or two later, Joe had called at the flat, and found her on the floor, haemorrhaging. I suppose our behaviour that night – mine and Joe's, was totally predictable.

A couple of days later, I left Cookie's house where I was staying, and went with her and Cherry to the hospital. Joe was sitting in the waiting room, munching french fries and KFC out of a carton. Neither of us spoke. Then Joe pushed the carton of chicken across the table, and told me to take some. I did. Then we both went in and sat with Loretta until she died.

Inside the cemetery most of the stones are black marble, with fine gold lettering. I like the homemade efforts best. The rough wooden crosses that you see here and there, with 'Mam' or 'Dad' painted on them in thick white letters.

Loretta has a cross like that, though we are saving up for a stone. Right now her grave has a blanket covering of long brown pine needles over it. Fallen from the pine tree overhead. There's a row of tall pines all along this side of the cemetery – and I see them differently now, depending on the season.

It's late spring and the sky is blue and the sun is shining. Looking up at the patch of blue, through the pines, I notice the little wooden pine cones, tucked beneath the brush of feathery green branches. 'Like little brown eggs,' I say to Chip-chip as we walk away. Chip-chip says it takes two years for these pine cones to mature and fall, as they're doing now, all around us as we walk. Two years! I think to myself, well, that must be about right.

'Hey! Frank Sinatra's dead,' says Chip-chip, as we reach the exit gate. 'Is he?' I say without thinking. 'Then his arse must be cold.' At first, Chip-chip is shocked, then he starts to laugh. 'That's your mother talkin' that is,' he says. 'That's Loretta!'

'Yeah,' I say looking at him and smiling. 'I think it is!'

THE LAST JUMPSHOT

Xtra practice? say the old laggers, the old leg timbers Parish and
Bo. You mean xtra on top of xtra?

Well, practice makes perfect, I point out cheerfully. And
anyway, Coach wants us there. For one last run-out.

S'all right for you – Captain Fantastic.

Yeah, Mr Campbell Jones!

But what about us, man? says Chip. We're whacked out.

No! No! I got plenty left in the tank, says Id, the Valleys Boy.
Let's go for it!

Silence.

I vote we go for it—?

Everyone looks at the white boy 'gone off'. As if they've just
been dealt a kick to their collective sensitivities.

Then Chip-chip jumps to his feet, suddenly re-energised,
resurrected, almost. Yo, let's go, he says, breezing past Id #1, as
if Id #1 had never spoken. Come on guys, what're we waiting
for, yeah?

The guys jump up. Yo, let's go!

Great, I say. Now we're all agreed.

Bouncing the orange basketball I follow them out of the flat,
thinking, smiling. It's because of me that Idris #1 got involved
with the A team in the first place, along with his sub and
namesake Idris #2. I recommended them to the new Coach,
Mulrooney. The two Ids, bible-black and paper-white. Outside
competition. Works like clock.

Standing by the bus stop. Waiting. Fooling around, waiting, in
an afternoon sun that gives off plenty of light, but no heat. Maybe
it's too late for heat this time of year. Even so, we six black guys

(one honorary) standing on the green hill, under the lone, battle-scarred bus shelter must appear potent. Sunlit. At least in the sunken eyes of elderly shoppers on the supermarket free-bus, which hoves into view before we've been standing there five minutes.

Hey look what's coming, says Chip. *FAZZDERS!*

And the guys start yelling *fazzder! fazzder! fazzder!* as the bus crawls up the hill. The uniformed peaked cap behind the wheel looks as though he'd like to drive straight past. But we step out into the road, all six of us and flag him down. A shade uncool for young gods lately fingered by the sun, agreed. But we can brazen this out. Easy. After all, why pay more, as *FAZZDER* says?

Thank you, driver!

Yeah, thanks, drive!

You boyz all goin' shoppin'?

We are, drive, says Chip. Gonna buy... washing powder. Ain' we, guys?

S' right, yeah. Big bogzz size!

Inside the bus, the chit-chat drops to a murmur as we crowd on board. Then a few bold whispers follow us up. Whispering, all the way up the winding stairs: look... look how many... Somalis?

Innit Somalis?

All praise be to God I say, seeing the upper deck empty; like a breath of fresh air.

Old fogies. Though that type of misidentification doesn't bother me at all. Because I'm secure in my Keltic black heritage, come whatever? But it riles the hell out of Parish and Bo, because Parish and Bo are Docks. And being 5th or 6th generation Docks Boyz (from 'Old Doggz' as they kindly explain to the rest of us) means being black in a way that is knee-high to royalty. At least the way they tell it. Though Lisha – who knows – reckons the nearest Parish and Bo come to being royal, is when they're sat on their butts in the Big Windsor holding forth. There the guys get serious admiration and respect (from flocks of daredevil scribes, tourists and whatnots) simply for sitting and being: Old Doggz.

Which is why they feel particularly hurt now, and aggrieved.

D'fuckin dee-crepts, says Bo. I'd like to punch their lights out. One by one.

Yeah, dee-crepts, says Parish. One arf of em are wearin NHS eye glass an they still carn see! I mean, do I look *Zomali, me?*

The two Ids seated down the front of the bus throw a quick look back. Then they make cartoon-type eyes at one another, and burst out laughing. *Zeeong!*

Oi, shouts Bo. What you got to laugh about, *Warrior Boy?*

The cut in his voice is directed at Idris #2, who is indeed Somali, and very tall timber. Which fact perhaps Bo has forgotten as Id is seated. Now the Somali boy shoots his long legs from under the seat and thunders down the aisle of the bus.

I'm Warsangeli, he yells, right up in Bo's face. You get it right, OK? Warsangeli Welsh!

Guys, I raise my hand peaceably. Let's all remember we're a team, OK?

The only response to this is a simmering, mutinous silence.

And then my mobile goes off. And suddenly everyone is transfixed as this wondrous new ringtone hits the air.

Orr, man, now that is just—just—

Awwsome, supplies Id #2.

Aye, *awwsome!* agrees Bo. I mean, d'fuckin US Cavalry Charge?

S' what they use on the NBA clockshot, innit? says Id.

Correct, Mr Hassan. Grinning, I let the mobile play on, unwilling to break its spell. And when Lisha gives up and rings off, the famous US bugle call continues to root and toot in our headspace. Like mood music. Linking us, each and every one of us six guys sat there on the *FAZZDA free-bus,* to the place where we know we wanna be, which is Planet NBA!

Though the bus actually drops us off at the out-of-town shopping complex. And while the pensioners shuffle forward with their bags and four-wheel trolleys, we're down the stairs, off the bus and out, into the sunshine. Green fields. The guys look round. Birds and shit. For them, this is always, *always,* the back of beyond. But not for me, I grew up here. I'm Pontprennau through and through.

Dotted across the fields are the familiar black and white splotches, sturdy young calves chewing up the grass. It's like those pretty pictures you get on cartons of *Ben & Jerry's* ice cream. Except that these are male, Bobbi calves and therefore useless for dairy; but great for kebab meat. Nowadays donner kebab is all these big-eyed spindly legged guys are good for, apparently.

So it's Friday afternoon still. And very late in the afternoon for some of us, standing around courtside, kitted up and ready to go. At only 5 feet 8 inches tall, and with the *Big Two O* approaching fast, it's beginning to dawn on me – that I'm only growing older, not taller. While lags like Parish and Bo are even further down the hill.

But right now? Our spirits are sky. Keyed. Because incredibly, this last-minute run-out has coincided with a VIP visit. Up and coming Councillor Ms Susannah somebody, has turned up here at the sports centre (actually a discontinued warehouse) with a TV camera crew in tow.

And while the Councillor lady and Coach Mulrooney talk to the cameras about disaffected youth and the need for *blah blah blah,* we await the whistle. Excited, expectant and more than ready to roll. Then, unfortunately the Councillor lady trips over her tongue, and starts talking about *disinfected* youth. And they have to start over again.

Orr, man!

The guys fall out, and begin to goof around a little.

Hi there, whispers Chip, pretending he's on camera. My name is Michael Jeffrey Jordan an I'm not *disinfected,* bold-assed bitch. Y'hear? I'm still catchin!

Yeah, he's catchin, he's catchin—

An we catchin!

Orr, c'mon guys, behave—

OK. Hi, I'm Kobe, whispers Id the Valleys Boy. And everyone cracks up laughing.

Including me. Until I note that Coach Mulrooney, all black beetling eyebrows and Irish-American red face, is looking hard across the floor. At us, at me? Immediately I'm reminded of the need to keep a serious head on here. I mean, once we get to London and tomorrow's final – who is to say who's out there? Watching? But for now Coach Mulrooney, the man who successfully rebranded us from the Karbulls to the Crows (post-9/11) is calling the shots.

OK guys, let's keep it down, now, I say briskly. Just 24 on the clock, and it will be the *Big One!*

Yeah!

When Kardiff Crows go toe to toe with the London boyz.

D'cocker knee boyz?

Yeah, d'cocker knee boyz! Suddenly I slam the air with my fist and yell out loud: Hey, no con-test!

At last Coach Mulrooney blows his whistle. That heart-stopping shriek. And for half a nanosecond I freeze – like a five- year-old, back on the school playground. Until I break free, shake free from the loop of time and go charging forward—

Great shot there, Campbell! shouts Coach Mulrooney, as we go three on three for the cameras, and I make the first basket.

Great jumpshot!

Then everything spools forward for me. Faster and faster. And despite my best efforts to play it cool, (keep it for tomorrow, play it cool) I'm suddenly on fire. Smoking. The heat is in the house, as they say. And what a fantastic house it is! This echoey space we're running in; this *huge* aluminium-walled warehouse, that we still call Goodz 4-U. Once it housed an empire of wonderful, wonderful things: like Nike Classic, Air Force, Converse, Zoomerific; and the sneakers I favour today, which are Jumbo Lift-Off.

And again, we have lift-off, because I'm playing out of my skin!

136

Hey where's the D? shouts Coach Mulrooney, abruptly switching sides. Watch Campbell! he shouts in irritation. Stop *Soup* Campbell! (Is *Soup* some jokey kind of put-down, I wonder, designed to halt my flow?) Too bad if it is. And too late. My feet push off the ground, my arm comes up. I grab the orange rock and it's a steal.

They're stealing it! cries Coach Mulrooney. *They are stealing it!* As Id #1 and I rotate the glowing orange rock between us. Tossing it back and forth, back and forth between us. Like a magic ball on invisible string. Invincible as we gallop up court for the nth time. Throwing a fake on Parish, throwing a fake on Chip. We thunder for the line, dropping Bo's D-fence for dead, as Id #2 pops up on the inside. And I toss the ball to Idris, that tall Somali timber. And get it back *smack!* as I run into space and stop. Right foot slam on the edge of the paint.

All at once, the famous US bugle call rings through my head. Fifteen seconds I calculate coolly, or one last jumpshot. And everyone out there will know who I am. I will alchemise my name Campbell Jones. ID-ing it. Gold-plating it to *Campbell*. Period. Aka the Can Man, aka the first Welsh Black who is destined to blaze a trail through the NBA!

The Bible tells us that your old men shall dream dreams, while your young men shall see visions. And when I finally make the shot, the ball leaves my hands and soars through the air. Like a vision. Spinning into space, like a dazzling orange sun that arcs, then fades. Drops and fades... fades... fades. Until... hey, hey hey! *It's BIG BASKET and another three pointer!*

But, I thought I caught a sound back there? As the ball dropped on its way through hoop and net. *It hit the rim.* It hit the rim! So naturally, I have to try again. And again. Leap on the glowing ball and try again. For the perfect throw, the perfect throw. Until united to a man, the guys grab a hold of my arms, just to make me stop. Stop! Then Coach Mulrooney comes rushing up, and thrusting his angry red peasant face right in front of my eyes, he screams: *Are you crazy, or what?*

I suppose crazy must be the answer. No question. Because when he tells me I'm relegated to the bench for tomorrow's final, all I can think to do, right there in front of the cameras, the Councillor lady and everyone, is to throw my head back. Right back, and just... bellow out my misery, like a bull calf in a field. Then bring my head down hard, in a replicating action and nut the guy... and nut the guy... and nut the guy...

Francesca Rhydderch's début novel, *The Rice Paper Diaries*, was longlisted for the Authors' Club Best First Novel Award and won the Wales Book of the Year Fiction Prize 2014. She was also shortlisted for the BBC National Short Story Award for her story 'The Taxidermist's Daughter'. She co-edited *New Welsh Short Stories*, and her English translation of the modern Welsh-language classic *Tywyll Heno* (Dark Tonight) by Kate Roberts will be published in 2018. She is currently Associate Professor of Creative Writing at Swansea University.

Joan Baker was born in Cardiff in 1922. She studied at Cardiff College of Art, where she taught from 1945 until 1983. She exhibited regularly and her work is in several public collections. Her earlier paintings included carefully observed figure groups but after the 1960s she concentrated on coastal and woodland landscapes. She painted *Warm and Cool* in about 1960. It records a corner pub near the Art College in Cardiff. Four people seem to be oblivious of one another. One man walks by, head down, and another is solitary at the bar. The woman waiting patiently near the open door is, the artist has said, 'selling her wares'. Only the well-dressed woman with a shopping basket seems to be looking out into the world.

Peter Wakelin

LIBRARY OF WALES

The Library of Wales is a Welsh Government project designed to ensure that all of the rich and extensive literature of Wales which has been written in English will now be made available to readers in and beyond Wales. Sustaining this wider literary heritage is understood by the Welsh Government to be a key component in creating and disseminating an ongoing sense of modern Welsh culture and history for the future Wales which is now emerging from contemporary society. Through these texts, until now unavailable or out-of-print or merely forgotten, the Library of Wales will bring back into play the voices and actions of the human experience that has made us, in all our complexity, a Welsh people.

The Library of Wales will include prose as well as poetry, essays as well as fiction, anthologies as well as memoirs, drama as well as journalism. It will complement the names and texts that are already in the public domain and seek to include the best of Welsh writing in English, as well as to showcase what has been unjustly neglected. No boundaries will limit the ambition of the Library of Wales to open up the borders that have denied some of our best writers a presence in a future Wales. The Library of Wales has been created with that Wales in mind: a young country not afraid to remember what it might yet become.

Dai Smith

WWW.THELIBRARYOFWALES.COM